RED FLIGHT TWO

Milton Dank

RED FLIGHT TWO

7876

Delacorte Press/New York

Published by
Delacorte Press
1 Dag Hammarskjold Plaza
New York, N.Y. 10017

Manufactured in the United States of America

First printing

Library of Congress Cataloging in Publication Data

Dank, Milton, [date of birth]
    Red flight two.
    Summary: A brave young officer of the Royal Flying
Corp witnesses the devastating effects of World War I
while serving with a group flying the newly developed
Sopwith Camels.
    [1. World War, 1914–1918—Aerial operations—Fiction.
2. Air pilots—Fiction.] I. Title.
PZ7.D228Re   [Fic]   81-176
ISBN 0-440-07336-7   AACR2

For Stefan, Daniel, and Jacob

1

With the cunning and skill of a seasoned hunter, the pilot stalked his unsuspecting prey through the cloud-filled sky. The late afternoon sun was low, and by keeping it always behind him as he weaved among the billowy cumulus, he closed unseen on the khaki-colored plane ahead.

Ten thousand feet—almost two miles—below were a rugged coastline, chalk cliffs, a sprawling town, and the Channel, shifting from a light green near the beaches to the cool aquamarine of deep water. On a hilltop overlooking the town stood the ruins of a Norman castle surrounded by a crazy patchwork of fields and woods splashed with the bright colors of autumn. Had the pilot looked away from his relentless pursuit, he would have seen a faint dark line on the eastern horizon that was France. And if he had not been deafened by the engine and slipstream noises, he would have heard the unceasing rumble of the guns on the Western Front. By early October 1916 this drumbeat of the war had been sounding for two years and two months. It never stopped.

But he heard nothing except the blood pounding in his ears and saw nothing but the tiny brown-green biplane slipping in and out of view among the clouds. Every muscle, every fiber of his being, was intent on closing the distance, on getting unseen within firing range of his intended victim.

A slight back-pressure on the stick sent his plane skimming up over a cotton-wool mountain, and he hung there just long enough to calculate the quarry's distance, speed, and direction. Then he slipped back into the valleys of light and shadow between the towering cumulus. Only a slight correction in heading was needed to intercept the plane ahead. He knew exactly where the other plane would be in two minutes, where it would enter the break between the clouds and give him a clear shot at minimum range.

The blind fool! Edward thought. He hasn't seen me yet. Keeps looking from side to side, but never behind him.

Reaching over the windshield, he pulled the cocking handles of the two black Vickers machine guns that jutted forward menacingly along the top of the cowling. It was a familiar action, one he had performed many times just before plunging into a dogfight. He never allowed himself to consider what ammunition at six hundred rounds a minute could do to wood, fabric, wire, and steel tubing—much less dwell on its effect on flesh and bone. Once he had worried about those things, and it had broken him.

When the khaki plane bearing the insignia of the Royal Flying Corps emerged from behind a cloud and flew into the clearing, Edward's plane was only eighty yards behind it and slightly below, flying a parallel course. He was in a perfect position, right in the blind spot of the unwary pilot ahead. Now, look as he might, the hunted man could never have spotted death lurking under his tail. Cold meat, Edward thought. Serves the idiot right.

His right hand gripped the control stick tightly as his thumb crept forward to the firing button. As the range closed to fifty yards the red, white, and blue stripes on the tail of the khaki plane were in the center of his gunsight, and still the unsuspecting pilot did not turn, climb, or dive.

Now! Edward pressed the firing button firmly and braced himself for the familiar yammering of the machine guns.

Instead there was a loud click as the firing pins slammed forward into empty chambers. The engine roared as Edward pushed the throttle wide open and climbed sharply alongside the "dead" plane. The other pilot, his face white with fear under his helmet and goggles, stared in amazement at the plane that had appeared so suddenly off his left wing.

Edward glared across the narrow gap at the frightened face, then with a commanding gesture jerked his thumb over his shoulder in the direction of the airfield. *You're dead. See if you can find your way back to the field and we'll bury you.*

Without waiting for an acknowledgment from his crestfallen "victim," Edward banked his plane sharply to the left and dove straight down through the clouds. He thrust his face out into the biting slipstream, letting the cold rush of air cool his feverish mind. His hands were trembling on the stick as he thought of the fury that had gripped him as he pressed the trigger. It was more than just anger at an inept student; it was the frenzy that always appeared in aerial combat. He knew it well.

The airspeed needle quivered about the red danger line, but he sat rigid, staring straight ahead. His mind was filled with bits and pieces of a dozen dogfights in the skies of Flanders: Brightly painted planes twisted in the frantic acrobatics of the war in the air. Some exploded and burned; others spun down lazily, a dead hand on the stick. Above the roar of wide-open engines he could hear the stutter of machine guns and see the yellow tracers . . . then flames and oily black smoke. . . .

With a start, Edward saw the ground rushing up at a terrifying speed The taut fabric of his wings rippled as they twisted slightly under the strain. Instinctively he eased the plane out of its dive, leveling off at five hundred feet. Off to his right he saw the narrow blue line of the Royal Military Canal and followed it to the airfield.

*   *   *

The adjutant stood in the doorway and announced, "Lieutenant Burton to see you, sir." There was a note of apology in his voice.

Major Henderson, commanding officer of the Advanced Flying School at Shelbourne, groaned in anguish. He hurriedly signed the papers in front of him and slid them under the blotter on his desk. Only then did he mutter resignedly, "Send him in, Captain." Reaching into the empty left sleeve of his tunic, he scratched the stump of his arm—a memento of a dogfight over Ypres last winter. It seemed to itch worse whenever Burton came storming in.

Before the adjutant could summon the visitor, Edward pushed past him, came to attention before the desk, saluted impeccably, and said, "Sir! Lieutenant Burton has permission to speak to the commanding officer!"

The major winced and leaned back in his chair as if to escape the loud, angry voice. He brushed his forehead casually with his forefinger to acknowledge the salute and braced himself for the inevitable tirade. "Yes, Burton, what is it?" His voice carried the weary conviction that he knew what it was and had heard it many times before. What a firebrand this boy is, Henderson thought as he contemplated the tall, erect lieutenant-instructor in front of him. It must be his American blood.

When Burton had first reported to the flying school, the major had welcomed him eagerly. Instructors with combat experience were rare—

there was always a shortage of pilots at the front —and Edward had impressive credentials. One of the first to go in 1914, he had seven victories in the air, had been decorated and mentioned in dispatches. True, he had had a nervous breakdown, but after almost two years of combat flying that was not unusual. Burton looked like a flier: tall, with black hair, a thin straight nose, and a square stubborn chin. And the major's snap judgment had proved correct, for Edward was an outstanding instructor.

Edward wasted no time in coming to the point. "I will not pass Lieutenant Evans for duty with an operational squadron."

The major stared. By God, this was more than the usual carping about "inadequate training" and "sending green men to face German veterans." This was damn close to insubordination.

"I don't understand, Burton. As you know, Evans was posted this morning for shipment to France. I've just signed the orders and he is to leave tonight with six other new pilots who have completed the advanced course. According to his record—which you filled out, I might add—he's not too bad a flier. Not brilliant, but certainly average. May I remind you that it is the senior staff who decide when a man is qualified for active duty—not lieutenant-instructors who have been here only two months?"

"Two months here as an instructor, sir, but twenty-two at the front. I think I know when a student is ready."

"See here, Burton," the major interrupted, "we

have found that instructors who are just back from operational squadrons tend to shelter their students too much, always wanting to give them more and more training before qualifying them. In the short time you have been at this school, you have shown that tendency to an alarming degree, always complaining, always demanding more time for instruction. It is for that reason that the senior staff alone decides when a new man is ready."

"Major," Edward pleaded, "please listen. I took Evans out this afternoon for a mock combat. I told him to look for me at ten thousand feet above Rye Bay and, as soon as he spotted me, to rock his wings and come straight at me. Sir, he never saw me! He wandered around the sky, forgetting to keep turning, to change altitude, or to look behind him. The man has no air vision—he's blind up there. He'll be dead in a week if you send him to the front!"

Henderson shifted nervously in his chair and stared gloomily at the papers on his desk. This was not a job for a man who had led the highest scoring squadron in France less than a year ago, a pilot with six victories. Still, someone has to do it, Edward knew, which is probably what the fool who wrote the order for the Charge of the Light Brigade said to himself.

"What you don't understand, Burton," the major said, "is how serious the situation at the front is right now. Our losses in the air have been appalling this last month. Pilots are desperately needed. . . ."

"Pilots, yes," Edward implored, "but Evans and the others are of no use in the air—unless we're interested in fattening the list of German victories. Evans has more time in a fighter plane than any other student here—I've seen to that—but even he has only ten hours solo! Ten hours! My God, sir, he can't even do a loop without falling into a spin. Sending him to France now is murder!"

"That will do, Lieutenant," Henderson said sharply. "You're forgetting yourself. The orders are signed. Evans and the others leave tonight. They'll have to take their chances over the lines as we all do—or did." He glanced at his empty left sleeve.

Edward caught the look on the C.O.'s face and was silent. A wave of guilt swept through him as he remembered that, unlike the major, he might fly in combat. He was almost nineteen—a prime age for a flier and an experienced combat pilot. Yet he was here at the flying school, teaching other men how to fight, rather than serving with a squadron in France. And the reason for his absence from the fighting made him ashamed. He knew that no one blamed him, but still he blamed himself.

Five months before, Edward had seen his best friend, Iain Ogilvie, leap to his death from a burning plane, a ghastly sight that had never left him. Edward was a broken man after that. "Combat fatigue," the doctors called it, and they kept him in the base hospital for two months before returning him to England on convalescence leave. It had been Iain's sister, Ann, and father who had taken him in and restored him to health. But the trembling in his hands and legs had never left him completely. In the air when the strain was greatest, it still came back and reminded him of the limits of his endurance. At the end of his leave the examining board had sent him to Shelbourne as an instructor. They were polite and complimentary, talking of his long service in the air, his youth, and his citations for valor, but the implication was clear: he could never again be trusted to serve at the front.

Major Henderson was watching him closely. Edward started to protest again, but seeing the C.O.'s stony face, he was silent. No point to it now, Edward thought. Henderson hates this business as much as I do—and is just as helpless to stop it. Even if he were mad enough to countermand the orders, the War Office brass would simply relieve him and send Evans and the others out as quickly as possible. It's this insane war.

"Sir," Edward said finally, "I'm turning in a negative report on Evans. I can't stop his being sent to the front, but I want this protest in the files."

The major nodded. "That's your privilege, of course. Submit your report within the hour. Dismissed."

Edward saluted, turned sharply on his heel, and marched out of the office. His face was flushed with the chagrin of his failure. All his life—at school and in war—he had hated to fail. No one at Falkland School knew that better than his closest friend, Colley Evans. On the playing field, Edward and Colley had competed fiercely and still remained the best of friends, each respecting the strength and determination he had found in the other. Colley had been killed ten months ago leading a raid on a German trench. Tonight his younger brother, Tommy, would leave for France and Edward was helpless to prevent it.

The adjutant looked up quickly as Edward came out of the C.O.'s office. Then he busied himself with his paper work. The walls were thin and he had heard everything, but being a wise man with long army experience, he knew better than to comment or try to joke about the situation. Edward picked up two copies of the standard report form from the pile next to the door and walked out of the headquarters building.

He was in his spartan room writing the report and feeling miserable about it. What's the point? he asked himself. Tommy Evans would go to France no matter what Edward did. There would be no time for additional training over there. He would be sent into action at once. Anyone who can fly goes into the fight even if he can't do a decent loop. Tommy Evans would be an easy victory for some German veteran, and there was nothing that could be done about it.

As he signed his name at the bottom of the form he was conscious of someone standing in the doorway, shuffling his feet. But Edward did not look up. He folded the report, sealed it carefully in an official envelope, then addressed it. He knew who was standing there, and he dreaded the conversation that was about to take place.

Finally he put the envelope in the drawer of his table and said, "Come in, Tommy."

Tommy Evans came in hesitantly, unsure of his reception. He stood almost at attention in front of the table, a contrite, even guilty, look on his face. Like a schoolboy, Edward thought, waiting for punishment. The schoolboy Tommy had been only six months ago. Damn it, why hadn't he stayed at Falkland where he belonged instead of rushing to enlist as soon as he was of age? But then, why didn't I?

"I was pretty bad up there, wasn't I, sir?" Tommy's voice was soft.

Edward took his time, searching for the right words. Tommy was so much like his older brother: middle height, muscular, the same sandy hair, blue eyes, and ruddy complexion. Colley had been a bit taller and not as handsome, more rugged, more a man even at sixteen. How long would Tommy last at the front? How long before his parents got another crushing telegram? *"The War Office regrets to inform you that your son . . . gallant and determined attack . . . for King and Country."*

Shaking his head to clear it of ghosts, Edward said, "You were pretty bloody awful. If I had been a Jerry, you would be dead by now." Tommy cringed at the cold words, but Edward knew that this was not the time for softness or vague generalities. Tommy had to learn fast. "How many times have I told you to keep your head turning, up, down, front, back—especially back, especially into the sun? That's where they'll come from, because you can't see them until the last moment."

"I thought I spotted you once," Tommy said eagerly, "but you disappeared so quickly that I decided it was a shadow on the clouds. The light was awfully tricky. I was afraid of looking like a fool if I took evasive action because of a shadow."

"Better a live fool than a dead hero." As soon as he said it, Edward regretted the words.

Tommy nodded and stared at the floor. "Like Colley, you mean?"

"Sit down, Tommy. Use the bed. They don't give us chairs for visitors, I'm afraid."

Tommy sat gingerly on the edge of the bed and rubbed his cheek slowly as he struggled to ask the all-important question. When he finally did, there was a slight quaver in his voice. "Are you going to fail me for what happened this afternoon?"

Edward shook his head. "No, Tommy. I wanted to keep you here another week for more air work, more simulated combat, but they need you desperately in France. You leave tonight with the others."

The smile that lighted the younger man's face— he was barely eighteen—was so joyful and excited that Edward turned his head to hide his own pain. *He still thinks it's some great glorious adventure.* Tommy had only an hour or so before leaving, and Edward had to get him ready—no, not ready, he would never be that, but at least warn him and perhaps give him a chance to learn the tricks that old pilots know instinctively. Tommy would see his friends die as Iain had died, as Colley had died—if he lived long enough.

"It's not what you think, Tommy. . . ."

"I'll be all right, sir. Honest I will. Once I'm in action, it will be fine. I was never very good in school, couldn't stand being preached at, if you know what I mean, but I always did well outside the classroom. Don't worry about me. I'll be fine and I won't let you down."

Edward tried to smile at the boyish enthusiasm, but he could only manage a sickly grin. He felt a hundred years older than Tommy.

"Of course you'll be all right, Tommy, and I'm certain that you'll do us proud. You're not a bad flier"—that was a lie, a necessary lie—"just inexperienced, but that makes all the difference in a dogfight. It's the man who is more alert, who sees the other plane first, who knows how to gain the advantage of speed and altitude and can turn more tightly, who survives. So I want you to listen carefully to what I'm about to say. I've said it to you before many times, but I want you to hear it again—and to remember it."

He started a long speech filled with technical terms about engine power settings, rate and angle of machine-gun fire, interception courses, escape spins, Immelmann turns for gaining altitude— everything he had learned in twenty-two months of air fighting. All the little tricks that made the difference between living and dying. The clock on the table was ticking loudly. Time was running out for Lieutenant Thomas Madsen Evans, and only Edward knew it.

At first Tommy listened carefully, but as the technical data piled up he started to shift around uneasily and rub his cheek. His eyes wandered around the room and finally fixed on something above his instructor's head. Edward noticed the glazed look in Tommy's eyes. *Listen to me! I'm trying to save your life!*

When Edward once paused for breath, Tommy asked, "You were at the front for two years, weren't you, sir?" He was still looking away.

Edward turned slowly, searching for whatever it was that had riveted Tommy's attention. He found it hanging on the half-open door of a closet: his tunic, with the single line of brightly colored ribbons sewn by Ann above the breast pocket. Tommy was staring entranced at the Military Cross, the Distinguished Flying Cross, and the Mons Star. The hunger in the young man's face was painfully clear. Dreams of glory, Edward thought, the worst trap of all. If I warn him against glory-hunting, he won't listen. Why should he believe me? I felt just as he does now—but so long ago.

"I went out with Number Four Squadron shortly after the war began," Edward said. "I was seventeen—almost—and the RFC took me on as a mechanic and later as an observer. We flew Farmans and Avros, big cumbersome brutes, all struts and longerons and wires. We were lucky to get them off the ground and luckier still to get back alive. We saw our first action at Mons, then the Marne, Ypres, and a dozen other battles. We were the first squadron to mount a machine gun. My pilot, Iain Ogilvie, thought up the idea after a Jerry took a potshot at us with a rifle. Would you believe that we found him a week later and smashed his prop with one burst? Our first victory. We were very proud of that one.

"Later they sent me to pilot training school at Issoudon. My mother had tried to get me discharged as underage, but, instead of going home, I went to Paris and enlisted with the Canadians. After I got my wings, they sent me back, only now we were Number Twenty-four Squadron and there were not too many of the old-timers left. We flew Nieuport fighters on the Flanders front, protecting reconnaissance planes mostly. Iain Ogilvie was my flight commander"—and my friend, Edward thought wearily. Should I tell him how Iain died jumping out of a burning plane at three hundred feet? Shall I tell him that Iain, the bravest man I have ever known, had this terrible fear of burning to death and, devout Catholic though he was, kept a pistol in the cockpit to make certain it never happened? Better not. Tommy's going to need all his illusions.

"I was in the hospital for a while"—*my nerves gave way after Iain was killed, and I couldn't stop trembling*—"and was sent back to England on convalescence leave last July."

Edward stopped. His not talking about the dead seemed almost a betrayal of his lost friends, but he knew Tommy could not understand the grim reality, the brutal losses, and the pain of those who survived.

There was a long silence, and they sat quietly. Edward pressed his hands against his legs to keep them from trembling, while Tommy stared with undisguised longing at the ribbons on the tunic. *He sees himself walking down the Champs Elysées covered with medals and with a pretty girl on each arm. I see him under a crumpled mass of wood spars and canvas—if he's lucky enough not to burn.* Edward knew that his vision was closer to the truth. In the autumn of 1916 the average life-span of a new pilot on the Western Front had been calculated to be three weeks.

Edward could not take this charade much longer. "You'd better pack, Tommy," he said hoarsely. "You'll be leaving for the Dover ferry soon. Good-bye, and good luck."

Tommy stood up and offered his hand. "Good-bye, sir, and thanks awfully for everything."

They shook hands solemnly, and Edward tried to smile. "And, Tommy, just one last word."

"Yes, sir?"

"Try not to call lieutenants 'sir.' You're a lieutenant yourself now."

Tommy nodded. In the doorway he paused, turned, and said softly, "No matter what happens to me out there, Edward, always remember this: It will be better than dying in the mud of some filthy trench like Colley."

Then he was gone.

Edward sat motionless behind the table staring at the empty doorway. Tears swelled behind his eyelids. His heart was pounding, and there was a knot in the pit of his stomach. *The brave, gallant fool! Does it really matter how one dies?*

He took the envelope from the drawer and put it in his shirt pocket. Outside the hut an engine roared to life, and he could hear the muffled yells of the mechanics as they directed the pilot into position. Edward put on his tunic, adjusted the Sam Browne belt, patted the ribbons without thinking, and walked out of the room.

The light was fading fast as Edward walked across the tarmac, trying to sort out his thoughts. Losing Tommy was almost like losing Colley again, but there was nothing to be done. Perhaps this premonition of Tommy's doom was just a case of nerves. But Edward knew otherwise. Tommy Evans was not a good enough flier to survive the critical first weeks over the lines.

The adjutant looked up cautiously as Edward entered his office. "Yes, Burton?" The worried tone spoke volumes. One more outburst from the "Yank" and Major Henderson would tear a strip off everyone in sight—starting with his adjutant.

Edward reached for the envelope, then hesitated. Why? he asked himself. A bad report on his flying won't help Tommy and it won't help me. I can't escape this guilt with a piece of paper.

Aware of the adjutant's puzzled stare at his silence, Edward groped for something innocuous to ask. "What time do the new pilots leave for Dover?" he finally blurted out.

The captain glanced at a schedule on his desk. "The cars will pick them up in front of the mess

hall in twenty minutes and drive them to the railroad station."

Mumbling something about saying good-bye to
his student, Edward turned and left the office. As
soon as he was out of sight of the headquarters
building he took the envelope from his shirt
pocket, carefully tore it into bits, and scattered
the pieces in the air. At the same time he reached
a resolve toward which he had been groping all
afternoon.

Edward's diary for October 5, 1916:

> Tommy Evans left today for duty in
> France. He and the other new pilots were
> laughing and making bad jokes as they
> waited for the cars. Strange how they think
> they are immortal, and will continue to think
> so until one of them is killed. Then they'll
> have the sense to be afraid.
>
> I don't know how much longer I can go on
> teaching men to fly, then seeing them sent
> off to the front before they are ready. This
> feeling of guilt is unbearable. The only thing
> that will make it stop is to ask to be sent back
> into action. With my medical record it is
> unlikely that the War Office would allow me
> to go, but at least I would have tried.
>
> And if I did succeed, how would I explain
> this decision to Ann?

2

"Of course," Mr. Ogilvie said, "Guy Fawkes is not considered a traitor by everyone." He poured the sherry carefully into three heavy glasses and smiled at his daughter and her young man.

Standing by the window, Edward looked out at the street urchins in Belgrave Square accosting passersby and demanding "A penny for the Guy, sir?" It was a raw November day, and a dark, threatening cloud layer hung over the city, carrying with it a hint of snow. *No flying today, not with that ceiling. I hope it's the same at the front.* Edward felt a twinge of pain and regret at what he had to tell Ann and her father. It was certain to hurt them.

"You must remember, Edward," Mr. Ogilvie continued, "that we Catholics were terribly persecuted under James I, that unworthy son of the blessed Mary, Queen of Scots." The tall, gaunt, aristocratic Scotsman frowned as he recalled three-hundred-year-old injustices. "Fawkes was a soldier and a very brave man. Blowing up Parliament and the King was his way of defending the Old Faith. Well, let's drink to him, God rest his soul."

He handed around the glasses, smiling as if to deny the tension in the room. Ann accepted her drink without looking up. Since Edward's arrival she had been strangely silent, sitting quietly in the deep armchair, her eyes fixed on the fireplace. She knows, Edward thought unhappily. Somehow she has guessed.

At eighteen, Ann Ogilvie was a strong, determined young woman, tempered by the war as Edward had been. She was petite, with curly chestnut hair, a small nose slightly upturned at the tip, and large, intelligent brown eyes. Usually there was a humorous curve to her mouth, but now it was set in a line. Edward remembered the picture of her he had seen on Iain's dresser at the front. Was it really possible to fall in love with a girl from a photograph, or had that come later?

Dressed in the severe gray uniform of a nurse's aide, Ann sat tensely erect in the armchair. At Chelsea Hospital she helped care for the wounded soldiers and was spared nothing—the brutal sights of amputations, the empty eye sockets, the horrible whistling sounds made by men with chest wounds. She dutifully served long, backbreaking hours without complaint, for she was a soldier's daughter and a dead soldier's sister. But she hated the war. Ann and Iain had been very close, and when he was killed she had suffered deeply. Edward knew that he had taken Iain's place in her heart and that she feared losing him too. She would never accept his decision.

Edward took the glass from his host and sipped the amber liquid. "Fawkes was executed, wasn't he, sir? Rather horribly, if I remember my history books."

"The usual fate of anyone attempting the life of the King," Ogilvie said. "Hanged, then cut down while still alive, then drawn and quartered." He shook his head at the barbarity of the sentence.

Edward seized the opening boldly. "But he was a soldier—for his faith—and convinced that he was doing his duty?"

"Exactly right, my boy." The ex-major of the Royal Scots Fusiliers stiffened perceptibly and said, "That's what a soldier must do—always." It was the proud voice of a man who had served bravely in the Boer War and who had been wounded at the relief of Ladysmith. "That's what soldering means, doing one's duty no matter what the cost. But I don't have to explain that to you, Edward. You were one of the first to go in 1914. Twenty-two months at the front, Military Cross, D.F.C. I don't think I have to tell you what the soldier's code is."

Edward acknowledged the compliment with a vague nod. "But suppose Fawkes had been a different man. Suppose he had said, 'I've done enough for the cause. Let someone else risk his neck in this fight. I'll train them, give them the advantage of my experience, procure the gunpowder, and draw up the timetable. But when it comes to sneaking the charges into the cellar under Parliament and setting the fuses, well, I'll be far away and safe.' What would you think of that man?"

Ogilvie frowned and fiddled with his drink. Clearly he was upset by the trend of the conversation. He noticed that Ann was listening intently now, staring at Edward's flushed face. The concerned father took a moment to consider his answer. "I suppose I would think much less of him, but then that man's name would not be Guy Fawkes."

"No, I suppose not, but it could be Edward Burton." Ann started to rise from the chair, then sat back and set her lips tightly.

"My dear boy, this is—"

"Please, sir, let me finish." The words came in a rush now as all Edward's pent-up emotion broke loose. It was hard to say but it had to be said, and he wanted so desperately for Ann to understand. "For two months now I have been training men to fly and fight at the front, green youngsters, all of them brave and ignorant of what is ahead. I've had to stand by and watch them being sent out to the squadrons in France long before they were ready, knowing that they did not have a chance to survive out there. Do you know what that's done to me? How I feel about being safe far behind the lines—me, an experienced combat pilot— while half-trained fliers are being shot down by German veterans?" His voice began to break, and he stopped for a moment.

"Anyway, I couldn't take that anymore. I had to do something." *Now, say it now, even though it hurts her.* "Three weeks ago I asked to be sent back to my old squadron in France."

Edward watched Ann closely. She rearranged a stray lock of chestnut hair on her forehead and turned her head to stare once more into the fireplace, but not before Edward had seen the tears. Her fingers gripped the arms of the chair.

Mr. Ogilvie looked worried. "Are you certain this is a wise decision, my boy? After all, you came back from France in rather bad shape. To return so quickly to the fighting. . . ."

"You sound like the president of the examining board, sir. The Royal Flying Corps is not about to send me back to an operational squadron just because I want to go—machines cost too much money to entrust them to men who might break again under the stress of combat. No, they put me through a lot of tests, poking and probing, asking all sorts of fool questions about my dreams and how I got along with my parents."

He paused to get a grip on himself. The questioning had been more painful than he wanted to admit, even to himself. The board had made him relive the whole traumatic experience: Iain's death, the helpless, terrified feeling at seeing his best friend falling to his death, the tears, and then the blankness that had overwhelmed him. Edward remembered nothing about the flight back to the airfield. Fortescue and several others had lifted him from the cockpit. There had been soft, reassuring voices that he had barely heard as they hurried him to a car. A doctor had probed his body for wounds that did not exist. They had all been in his mind.

"The board was very sympathetic," Edward continued, "but I could see that they were doubtful about my ability to take any more combat stress. I'm certain that at least one spotted my hands trembling. In any case, I had my last interview yesterday."

There was a silence in the room as Mr. Ogilvie groped for something to say and Edward watched Ann fight to keep her composure. They could hear the servants moving about in the hall, getting ready for the evening meal. The only other sounds were the urchins' muted cries from the street and an occasional snap from the fireplace as a resin pocket popped.

Finally Ann asked quietly, "When will you know?"

Puzzled, Edward missed the thrust of the question. "Very soon, I expect. They need pilots, experienced fliers, in France. You do understand, don't you, Ann? I can't stay behind."

Ann paused for a moment, then said firmly, "No, I will never understand why you would do this to me—to us. First Iain, now you. Why?"

Edward stiffened at her tone. His fingers tightened on his glass, and when he spoke there was anger in his voice.

"You remember Tommy Evans, one of my students? He was posted missing on his third flight over the lines. I tried to keep him from being sent to the front before he was ready, but I failed. I won't be part of this crazy system that sends un-trained men out to be killed—and killed uselessly. That is the truth—I can't stand feeling guilty any longer."

"Will it help Tommy Evans and the others if *you* are killed?" Ann demanded. She put down her glass and rose from the sofa. "And you decided without asking me how I felt about your going back? Just your feelings, your guilt? Oh, Edward, that was too cruel!"

In tears, she ran from the room, leaving the two men staring after her. Mr. Ogilvie coughed in embarrassment. "I'm sorry, my boy. Unfortunate business."

"Is she right, sir?" Edward asked. "Am I wrong to want to do my duty as I see it?"

The older man shrugged his shoulders and sipped his drink. "I would not take all that too seriously. She's upset, you see. Doesn't want you back in the war. Ann and Iain were so close . . . having lost their mother when they were so young. She's never really accepted his death . . . too much of a loss, I suppose; and now you are going back. Too much for her. Give her time, Edward. She's a good, level-headed girl, but she needs time to work this out."

Edward nodded and put down his drink. "You'll understand if I don't stay for dinner, sir. I'd better return to the base."

"Of course, my boy, I understand perfectly. Call her in a few days after she has settled down." She won't, Edward thought, not now or later.

As they walked to the front door and the butler helped Edward into his military overcoat, Mr. Ogilvie was still chatting in an attempt to ease the pain he saw in the younger man's eyes. "That's terribly sad about young Evans, Edward. What happened?"

Edward looked up at the threatening sky. "Tommy's patrol was jumped by a full squadron of the new Fokkers. In the melee the old hands couldn't cover the new men—they were fighting for their lives. Tommy just never returned to the field. If we're lucky, we may find his grave somewhere during the next push. But more likely we'll never know."

"Perhaps he was taken prisoner," Mr. Ogilvie said in a somber tone. Edward shook his head. "The Jerries are very chivalrous about that. They would have dropped a message behind our lines if he had been taken prisoner—or if they had found his body. No, he's gone. Good-bye, sir."

Edward walked down the steps and across the square. A cold wind sent the leaves scurrying across his path, but he did not notice. He was thinking of Tommy's last words three weeks ago . . . "the mud of some filthy trench." *Please God, don't let him have died there.*

"A penny for the Guy, guv'nor?" A child with a dirty face, dressed in thin, shabby clothes, appeared in the twilight. Hand outstretched, but nervous and tense, he was ready for either a coin or flight. Edward grinned weakly and reached into his overcoat pocket for a shilling. The urchin gasped at the sight of the shiny silver.

"Here you are, old man," Edward said. "For the Guy—a brave man and a soldier."

Seizing the shilling eagerly, the boy turned to flee, then stopped and flung over his shoulder, "A filthy traitor, he was!"

Edward watched the small figure running across the square until it disappeared around the corner. *Well then, a brave man and a soldier and a traitor. It must be possible.*

He turned up the collar of his overcoat against the chill wind and hurried toward the railroad station.

He telephoned Ann every day for a week, but she refused to speak to him. Mr. Ogilvie was apologetic, clearly upset by her attitude. "She's been badly hurt, my boy. Give her a bit more time. She'll come around." Edward wrote long, pleading letters and sent her a copy of Robert Browning's love letters to Elizabeth Barrett, but there was no reply.

On the eighth day the adjutant called him in and handed him his new orders. The examining board had found Lieutenant Edward Burton physically fit for combat duty but strongly recommended that he not be sent to an operational squadron in France "because of his previous medical history, namely emotional problems that might be aggravated by service in the field." The War Office had therefore decided to send Lieutenant Burton to an air defense squadron near London. There he would help to protect the city against Zeppelins and German night bombers.

Edward would be releasing another pilot for the front.

He hated the idea of someone going in his place and let the hapless adjutant know it. "Not good enough for France, but they'll let me risk a machine flying around in the dark over London, dodging the balloon barrage and being fired on by our own guns. What kind of crazy sense is that?"

The captain sighed and shook his head. He could understand Burton's disappointment, but there was nothing to be done. "Sorry, Burton. The major telephoned to see if he could get the orders changed but it was useless. It seems that they have heard of your complaints about their training policy and you're not too popular just now up in Whitehall. They take a dim view of junior officers saying that we're sending untrained men to the front. You're lucky they didn't send you to Mesopotamia or some other Godforsaken spot."

The adjutant handed over an official-looking envelope. "Your orders. You report to Fawkes Green as soon as possible."

"Did you say *Fawkes* Green?"

"Yes, it's a new field just northeast of London. Why—is something wrong?" Edward shook his head and managed a grin. The coincidence struck him as half-amusing and half-ominous. "Any chance of a twenty-four-hour pass to take care of some personal business in London?"

"Sorry, Burton," the adjutant said, "the orders are quite explicit. No delay in reporting to your new post. Good-bye and good luck."

After he had packed his bags, Edward tried to reach Ann again. The butler said that she was out for the day. No, he did not know when Miss Ogilvie would return.

Lost in a vast, dark sea where sky and earth merged, the tiny plane climbed slowly toward the stars. Far below, the silver ribbon of the Thames twisted and coiled its way to the distant Channel. Not a light showed on the land as the British slept in the darkness of the blackout, one ear cocked for the menacing drone of German engines and the shrill warning of the air raid siren. Children still awake in their beds listened to the hum of the high-flying plane and wondered if it meant bombs again on the town.

Edward peered over the cockpit rim at the flickering blue flame of the engine exhaust. In the five weeks since he had joined Number Fifty-one Squadron, Home Defense Wing, he had learned a whole new set of rules for survival in the uncharted depths of the night sky. One of them was to watch the color of the exhaust flame to determine if the engine was performing correctly. But he must not stare at it, lest the bright light spoil his night vision.

In the middle of December, at ten thousand feet, the temperature was ten below zero. Even in his wool-lined flying suit, helmet, boots, and gloves, Edward shivered. He had to pound his feet against the floorboards to keep his toes from freezing. His head turned constantly, examining the gloomy depths of the sky in all directions. But the sky was empty. The plane droned through the night beneath the curved bowl overhead studded with stars. Was it another false alert?

An hour earlier, one of the numerous watchers along the Channel coast had telephoned headquarters, Home Defense Wing, to report the sound of engines approaching Southend-on-Sea from the east. Immediately the four nearest squadrons had been ordered to get their planes into the air and cover the paths that a Zeppelin might take to London. There had been no sighting by a ground observer before the planes took off, although there was a half-moon, but the searchlight and anti-aircraft gun crews had been warned of the possible approach of an enemy raider. Edward thought it also might be some training plane from the naval flight school at Dover or Margate on a night navigation flight—some student who had failed to report his intentions to Home Defense Headquarters. This had happened twice before to Edward—frozen because of some stupid cadet. Then again, it might really be one of the gasbags; it was a perfect night for a Zeppelin raid—high clouds, little wind, and enough of a moon to spot a target.

As he crossed over the curve in the Thames at Gravesend, Edward banked the plane on the northward leg of his search pattern. The heavy B.E. 12 responded slowly, as if reluctant to change course. For the thousandth time, Edward swore at the idiot who had selected the slowest observation plane in the Royal Flying Corps for the job of Zeppelin-hunting at night. They had built a cover

over the front cockpit, added a slightly larger engine plus a bigger fuel tank, and thought that this was the answer to the high-flying dirigibles. That the B.E. 12 could not fly higher than fourteen thousand feet, two thousand feet below the cruising altitude of their prey, did not faze the powers in the War Office. "Wait until the enemy descends to bombing altitude" was their reply to the pilots' complaints. But the enemy seldom did if he feared British planes about, preferring to drop his bombs from a safe height regardless of where they might land.

Useless to worry about that now. Better to concentrate on keeping this plane flying at this altitude and to keep from freezing. Edward shone his flashlight on the instrument panel to check his airspeed, fuel, and oil pressure. All okay. The beam glittered on a silver medallion nailed above the compass. Eighteen months ago, on Edward's first leave in London, Mr. Ogilvie had given him and Iain Saint Jude medals in the pious hope that the patron saint of those in peril of their lives would protect them. The other medal would be a melted glob buried in the mud of the riverbank in the charred remains of Iain's plane. Edward shivered at the thought and pounded his gloved hands together to keep the blood circulating.

The bitter cold brought another worry, Edward remembered as he carefully scanned the night sky. The only lubricant that would not freeze at these temperatures was castor oil, and several pilots had been stricken by its laxative effect while

inhaling the exhaust fumes. Not a very funny
thing to happen while tightly wrapped in flying
gear at ten thousand feet.

Fifteen minutes passed as the plane droned
steadily on the northern course. Far below he
spotted the glow from the boiler of a train speeding down to London. Thirty-five minutes of petrol
left. Another futile chase through the blackness
of an empty sky.

Suddenly, off to his left, two silver sword blades
split the night. Searchlights! The sound detectors
had picked up alien engines, and the powerful
beams were probing for the enemy intruder. Edward banked sharply and headed for the lights.
At the same time, he opened the throttle and began a shallow climb to maximum altitude. His
heart was pounding and there was a familiar
dryness in his mouth, both the well-known signs
of imminent action. If there was a Zeppelin
there, then Edward was between him and the
Channel, cutting off the enemy's escape route.
And if the gasbag was coming down to bombing
altitude, then Edward would be above him and in
perfect position for a diving attack.

The B.E. 12 climbed sluggishly in the thin air,
wallowing slightly from side to side. It took all
of Edward's skill to keep it from falling off on a
wing into a dive. Anxiously he watched the altim-
eter needle move slowly around the dial. Twelve
thousand feet. Still no sign of the Zeppelin, but
the searchlights had narrowed their search to the
northwest. The enemy must be coming from that
direction. Edward made a small course correction

to intercept the raider in the shortest possible time.

Twelve thousand five hundred. He was climbing at less than three hundred feet a minute. Once again Edward consigned some senior officer in Whitehall to the torments of hell. If the enemy spotted him before he was in firing range, the Zeppelin would immediately dump ballast and climb above him. Hurry up, you pile of junk, he swore under his breath, get up there fast and give me a chance to fire.

Thirteen thousand three hundred and the plane was wallowing badly. It would not climb much higher. Edward eased back the throttle and leveled off rather than risk falling into a spin if the B.E. stalled in the thin air.

Then he saw the Zeppelin for the first time. At ten miles' distance it was a tiny silver pencil that glittered as the searchlight beams caught and held it. All around the dirigible small red sparks flashed and disappeared as the antiaircraft guns opened fire. At that altitude—Edward estimated that the Zeppelin was cruising at twelve thousand feet—it would be pure chance if a shell fragment crippled the gasbag. So notorious was the inaccuracy of the A.A. guns that they were as likely to hit the B.E. 12 as the Zeppelin when Edward attacked.

The German captain, adroit at dodging the searchlights, led them a merry chase, slipping in and out of the beams as he navigated in a roughly southwest direction. Edward guessed that his target was the Royal Arsenal at Woolwich, about twenty miles up the Thames, and his heart beat faster as he realized that the enemy would have to hold his altitude to have a chance of hitting the concentrated buildings at the arsenal. *If he doesn't spot me until the last minute, I have a chance to make one pass before he gets above me.* He pulled back the throttle a notch, sacrificing airspeed to diminish the blue glow of the exhaust. Better to arrive a few minutes later, undetected. . . .

More searchlights joined the chase as the raider penetrated the second ring of guns and lights that encircled London. Now Edward could see the Zeppelin clearly—the two gondolas underneath that held the crew and the engines, even the dark circles on the top that were machine-gun pits. Up ahead, Edward spotted the big S-curve in the river. The arsenal was on the other side of the Thames, just past the curve. The crew in the gondolas was concentrating on the bombing run, but Edward knew that the machine gunners were searching the night sky for enemy planes. Two more minutes and he would be in position to attack.

They were two of the longest minutes in his life. Any second now he expected to see the Zeppelin drop ballast and rise up far beyond his ability to follow, escaping forever. But his luck held. As he reached his planned position, a thousand feet above the dark hulk and a half mile to the rear, the enemy machine guns were still silent. His right hand trembled on the stick and he gripped with his left hand to steady it. Soon the tremor disappeared.

Now! Edward closed the throttle and shoved

the control stick full forward. The whisper of the slipstream became a high-pitched scream as the B.E. dove at maximum speed toward the target. No need to hide now. The Jerries would know in a few seconds where he was. Edward fired a short burst from his machine guns to warm them, then thrust his head forward to peer through the telescopic sight.

The cross hairs of the gunsight divided the monstrous bulk of the Zeppelin just ahead of the tail fins. As the distance closed, Edward could see little dark figures in the gun pits, then tiny red spurts as the machine guns opened fire on the diving plane. In their surprise the enemy machine gunners had fired too soon, but in seconds the B.E. was in their range and Edward heard the hollow, popping sound of bullets whipping through the taut painted fabric of his wings. He hit hard right rudder and skidded the plane to one side to confuse the Jerries' aim. Then, at three hundred yards, he pressed the trigger on top of the control stick.

The B.E. shuddered as the Vickers gun on the left side of the fuselage and the Lewis gun atop the top wing chattered and bucked. Every fifth round was a tracer and every third round an incendiary. Some bright soul in the War Office, some desk-bound kiwi who had never flown in combat, had figured that this was the best choice for shooting down Zeppelins. And since the enemy dirigibles were filled with highly inflammable hydrogen, it made sense for once.

The bright yellow lines of tracers disappeared

into the gray skin of the monster. Edward, firing in short bursts to keep his guns from jamming, raised the nose slowly so that the bullets stitched their way up the back of the Zeppelin. He cringed as a wire broke on his left wing, then he dove straight down to put the gigantic tail fins between his plane and the deadly enemy fire.

As he sped past the rear gondola he caught a glimpse of tiny white faces peering at him. You or me, he thought grimly. Or some innocent civilians peacefully sleeping next to the arsenal. Damn you anyway!

Suddenly a torrent of water burst over his plane and splashed into the cockpit. For a second he had the terrible feeling that he had run into a waterfall and was about to be drowned, but he realized it was water pouring from the Zeppelin. The captain was lightening ship to escape the stinging wasp that threatened him. As he came out of the waterfall, out from under the protection of the Zeppelin's belly, the enemy tracers reached out for him again. Edward threw the B.E. into a steep bank and curved back for another attack. The enemy raider was rising rapidly, and soon it would be far above him. There was time for only one more pass.

Once again his guns fired and he could see his tracers riddle the area about the large Maltese Cross on the Zeppelin's side. But still nothing happened. "Burn, damn you," Edward shouted. Then the top Lewis gun stopped; its drum was empty. There would be no time for Edward to stand and

struggle to change the drum in the tearing slipstream. There were less than sixty rounds left
in the Vickers and the enemy was escaping rapidly. Edward kicked rudder and fired at the front
gondola, but missed. Then a searchlight caught
the two ill-matched duelists in its glare and the
Zeppelin disappeared into a blazing curtain of
light. Blinded, Edward swung away to avoid a
collision.

By the time he had regained his night vision
and circled back, the Zeppelin was two thousand
feet above him and still rising. It was hopeless.
The battle was over; the defender had lost. True,
the arsenal had been spared, but some coastal
town would now get the bombs intended for Woolwich. The Jerries would not take their damned
explosives all the way back to Germany.

Cold, wet, and exhausted, Edward flew in a
tight descending spiral toward his base. To have
come so close . . . to have actually fired on a gasbag . . . and then to see his bullets whistle harm-
lessly through the huge bulk of the enemy raider.
It was not only frustrating but shaming.

Seething with anger, he leveled out at two
thousand feet, picked up the familiar circular
reservoir that was his landmark, and flew straight
to the field at Fawkes Green. As soon as they
heard his engine the flare pots were lighted and
he spotted the fiery L that located the field. Not
bothering to recircle the landing area as regulations required, he closed the throttle and came in
fast, right down the long arm of the L. *Let the*

C.O. complain. I've had enough flying for one night.

The B.E. touched down smoothly, rolled to a stop, turned, and taxied swiftly through the tall grass toward the hangar line. Out on the landing strip the flares were being extinguished. There would be no more planes landing tonight. Edward was the last to report in.

In the yellow light of the acetylene lamps, Sergeant Christie looked gloomily at the B.E. in the corner of the hangar. "It's a risk, sir," he said mournfully. He liked Lieutenant Burton and had grown to admire him in the five weeks since the young pilot had joined the squadron, but what he was being asked to do struck the sergeant as aiding and abetting a suicide. "Even forgetting the damage your plane suffered tonight—three wires shot through, smashed longeron, holes in two main spars, not to mention a dozen rips in the fabric—this plane is very delicately balanced, you see. It's all worked out at the factory, and if we do what you ask . . ." The sergeant's voice dropped off, but it was plain that he foresaw disaster.

Edward persisted. "Look, Sergeant, our job is bringing down Zeppelins, right? Well, we can't do that as long as the damned gasbags fly several thousand feet above us. And the only way to get to them is to lighten the plane so she can climb higher."

"All perfectly correct, sir, but look what you're asking. A smaller gas tank. Removing the fire wall as well as practically everything in the cockpit that can be spared. Yes, the plane will be three hundred pounds lighter, but where will the center of gravity be, I ask you, sir? Who knows if the plane will fly straight with those changes?"

Edward grinned. "My responsibility, Sergeant. And, oh yes, take the Lewis gun and its mounting off the top wing. That will save a lot of weight."

Sergeant Christie's jaw dropped. "Does the lieutenant plan to attack Zeppelins with just one Vickers gun? If you'll excuse my saying so, sir, that . . ."

"Thank you, Sergeant, I knew that you would approve. And I want the incendiaries taken out of my gun belts on future flights. They're useless, worse than useless. Replace them with Mark I explosive rounds."

"Very dangerous that, sir. A faulty round might go off in the barrel. It's happened before."

"Let's hope it is more dangerous for the Jerries than it is for me, Sergeant. As soon as possible, please. I have a hunch that I'll have another chance at a Zeppelin before too long."

He left the hangar quickly before the sergeant could think of other objections to his plan. He was not at all certain that Christie was wrong, but something had to be done.

3

Edward's hunch was wrong. The next day, two days before Christmas, a winter gale swept down from the North Sea and kept all the planes in the hangars. Gusts of sleet mixed with snow pelted the airfield, and rime ice coated the wires that held the canvas sheds. Dark scud clouds driven by an icy wind fled across the sky. Far to the east, near Lake Constance on the German-Swiss frontier, the Zeppelins rested and waited for the weather to clear.

For a week the squadron moped and grumbled, trying to find some amusement to kill the long, tedious hours. Many of the pilots went down to London as soon as the day's flying was canceled, but Edward stayed in his hut, reading. To be in London and not to see Ann would have been too painful. He wrote a letter to the Evanses expressing his sympathy and the hope that Tommy was a prisoner. He wrote to the headmaster at Falkland School asking for news of his classmates—and dreading the reply. Then he wrote a cheerful letter to his parents in Philadelphia, full of amusing anecdotes about life in the squadron and assuring them that he was perfectly safe . . . "Zeppelins fly so high we can't get near them." His mother had gone to join his father in the United States three months ago to escape the loneliness and austerity of wartime England. Her letters to Edward suggested that his parents' reconciliation, after years of separation, had been successful and that she was even enjoying the quiet Philadelphia life. "I'm something of a celebrity here," she wrote, "having lived in England during the air raids. The people are wonderful, very kind and thoughtful, and insist on treating me like a heroine. I don't tell them how frightened I was."

He wrote long letters to Ann, trying to explain his decision to return to the war. There were no answers.

The weather worsened. Christmas Day was bleak as the snow piled up against the huts. Edward fought his way through the gusts, chilled by the freezing air even in his heavy overcoat, to check on Sergeant Christie's progress in modifying the plane. The crew chief was still unhappy about what he was doing and still predicting disaster, but orders were orders, and if Lieutenant Burton was willing to risk his neck to get a Zeppelin, the sergeant could only do his best to help him. The explosive rounds worried him most. Christie loaded the belts himself, not trusting the armorer to check every round.

Major Morgan, the squadron commander, stopped by to examine the work. He was silent as the plan was explained to him, shaking his head solemnly as the Lewis gun was dismounted. It was clear that he had little faith in the idea, but he had commanded a squadron in France not long ago and he knew that pilots had to be allowed to change their planes as they wished. Finally he left after giving only one order: The B.E. 12 was to be balanced and extra weights added if necessary to make certain it was stable in flight. After he was gone, Edward quickly countermanded the order. Extra weight would defeat the whole purpose of the changes.

New Year's Day 1917 dawned bright, clear, and cold. After a night of carousing the pilots dragged themselves from their beds to assemble in the mess hall for orders. Few had an appetite for anything but coffee and only groaned at the heaping plates of eggs and ham. Edward, who had skipped the drinking bout and wild antics, ate heartily. Excitement built in him as he watched the ground crews shovel the snow from the field to allow takeoffs and landings into the wind.

Standing in front of the assembled pilots, the major read the weather forecast: "Increasing ceilings and visibility. Winds less than ten miles an hour this afternoon and tonight. No precipitation for the next twenty-four hours." With the full moon tonight it would be perfect bombing weather. "Another freezing trip down the Thames," someone moaned.

Moonrise, the major continued, would be at 5:27 P.M., and the first patrol would take off at that time. They would be relieved in their assigned areas by the second patrol three hours later. "Except for Lieutenant Burton," the C.O. said with a frown, "who will take off at midnight, fly his patrol as usual, and return when his fuel is low." There was a burst of laughter at poor Edward's bad luck in drawing the midnight flight—the coldest and loneliest task of all. Still, if he insisted on going up with a small fuel tank . . .

Edward spent the rest of the morning checking his plane. Sergeant Christie showed him the results of the balance test, which indicated that the B.E. 12 was right on the edge of being unstable. The crew chief was worried that the decreased weight after firing all the ammunition would make the plane impossible to fly, but Edward pooh-poohed the idea and signed the acceptance sheet with a flourish. *Well, it's done. Now let's see if I was right or not. If I guessed wrong, I'll end up in a smashed crate on the mud flats of the Thames . . . with a broken neck, no doubt.*

He spent the rest of the day resting in his room, reading Rudyard Kipling's *Kim* for distraction. When he heard the engines of the first patrol warming up, he went out to the flight line to watch the takeoff. In the icy cold air, brilliantly lighted by the full moon, five planes stood wing tip to wing tip, blue flames flickering from their exhausts. Mechanics were swarming over them making last-minute adjustments, while out on the field other crewmen lighted the paraffin-filled buckets that lined the runway. It was an eerie scene but a familiar one.

Edward stood quietly shivering in the lee of a hangar as the B.E. 12s taxied out, roared down the cleared path, and disappeared over the trees. Now the field was strangely quiet and empty. He saw the major standing alone and thoughtful in front of his headquarters, staring into the night where his men had gone.

In the hangar Edward found Sergeant Christie still fussing over his plane. "Keep her here in the hangar until the last minute, Sergeant," Edward said. "I don't want any ice forming on the wings." Then he went back to his hut and stretched out on the bed. More than three hours to go. Waiting for the takeoff was always the hardest part.

The land far below was bathed in a soft silver light that clearly showed the snow-covered fields and the dark patches that were woods and villages. From fourteen thousand feet there was almost no sensation of motion. The landscape seemed to roll beneath the laboring plane at a creeping pace.

It had taken Edward forty minutes to coax the B.E. 12 to this altitude, fighting a tendency of the plane to fall off on a wing and dive down to denser, more hospitable air. Now it would go no higher, and reluctantly Edward eased back the throttle and leveled off. He glanced at the fuel gauge—already one-third of the precious petrol was gone. If he did not encounter an enemy airship in the next hour, it would be too late, for the remaining twenty minutes' fuel would just get him back safely to his home field.

Some high cirrus clouds drifted across the moon, surrounding it with a faint rainbow circle. Bomber's moon, Edward thought, remembering the popular superstition.

Suddenly he sat bolt upright and stared over the rim of the cockpit at the land below. As good pilots do, he had been noting the drift of his plane by the path it followed over the ground. It had been difficult from this height, but now he was certain that the wind had shifted and was blowing strongly from the southwest instead of almost due north. If the German captain became aware of this wind change before he reached the English coast, he would change course and make his approach to his target from the south to take advantage of the favorable wind drift. But Edward's course would take him north, away from the raider, and the second patrol was even now on its way home. The southern sector was unguarded.

Acting on his hunch, Edward banked the plane sharply and set a course south, letting the wind push him east toward the Channel coast. Excitement set in and he felt flushed despite the bitter cold. *There has to be a Zeppelin down there somewhere.*

The minutes passed as Edward anxiously searched the blackness of the night sky, looking for the telltale exhaust flames of the Zeppelin's engines. The needle of the fuel gauge crept down much too quickly toward the "empty" line, and once the plane's engine sputtered and missed, then roared again into life. Twenty minutes more and he would have to quit and head for home. *I can't hold this altitude much longer. This plane just wasn't built to fly this high.*

He had just opened the throttle slightly to feed more fuel into the carburetor when he saw the Zeppelin. Against the snow-covered ground the long, silver, cigar-shaped object was barely visible, but a moonbeam reflected off its skin into Edward's eye and pulled his head around. For a moment he thought it was a peculiar patch of ice on the ground, but then the dirigible moved across a dark wooded area and he saw it outlined perfectly. With a whoop of joy he turned to the attack.

The searchlights on the outskirts of London flared into life and began to probe the skies. Startled, Edward realized how close they were to the city. With this wind and heading he would not intercept the Zeppelin until they were over Lambeth, in sight of the Parliament building and Westminster Abbey. Too damned close, he thought, but can't be helped. I have to try to bring her down even if she falls on Buckingham Palace.

The moon was behind him, and he knew that the enemy machine gunners would spot him quickly. But changing course was out of the question. There was barely enough petrol left for five minutes' fighting, then he would have to break off or risk a forced landing in the dark on some strange farm field—or worse, in the center of London itself.

The Zeppelin was only three miles away and two thousand feet below its pursuer when Edward saw the shimmering threads of water appear below its belly. He had been spotted! The Germans were dropping water ballast to get above the threat that was fast approaching. *Not this time, Jerry,* Edward swore. *You won't escape again.* He made a slight course-correction to reach the point at which the enemy raider would pass through his altitude.

The gigantic bulk, a brilliant silver in the moonlight, came up to meet him. Yellow tracers whipped through the blackness, and Edward slipped the plane violently to the left to avoid the enemy fire. He reached forward and pulled the cocking levers on his machine gun and prayed that the cooling fluid had not frozen in the barrel. No time to warm his gun. Ten seconds to go.

He turned his head quickly and shut his eyes to avoid being blinded by a searchlight beam that had found them. *Damn that crew! Can't they see me here!*

Bam! A burst of red off to his right, then another above him. Edward cursed. *Not that too.* Unaware of the presence of a friendly plane, anti-aircraft gunners guarding the city had begun firing on the Zeppelin. *Just my luck if I'm shot down by our own guns.*

The Zeppelin was at his altitude now and still rising, but more slowly. Edward dove down beneath the huge tail fins and closed the throttle. Ahead he could see the dark teardrop shapes of the two gondolas, but this time there were no terror-stricken faces at the windows.

Selecting a point just to the rear of the front

gondola, Edward raised the nose of his plane slightly and pressed the trigger. The Vickers gun chattered in short bursts as he sprayed the belly of the Zeppelin, watching grimly as the line of tracers disappeared into the metal-colored skin. Between every tracer round, he knew, there were three explosive bullets, and he could imagine them striking the steel girders that were the Zeppelin's skeleton and exploding. His head was pounding and he kept swallowing nervously as he held the B.E. on the edge of a stall and fired again and again.

With a shudder the B.E., relieved of the weight of the ammunition, fell off on its right wing sharply and twisted down in a spin. Edward yelled with rage and whipped the controls over to counteract the diving turn, then kicked rudder. The plane responded sluggishly, as if reluctant to stop its descent into denser air, but finally the spin became a dive and Edward was able to ease the plane out to level flight. But he had lost four thousand feet. The Zeppelin was far above him, and he knew he could never get back to it in time. Tears of frustration fogged his goggles as he realized that he had lost again.

When finally the plane was under control, he looked up at the enemy now so far beyond his reach and cursed silently. Twice he had had the chance and twice he had failed.

Then he saw a reddish glow in the center section of the dirigible, faint at first, then growing and spreading and becoming brighter. Soon it filled the whole interior of the Zeppelin and Edward could see every girder in its framework. He stared at the strange sight.

Before his startled eyes the long, cylindrical airship broke in half and started to fall. From the pointed bow a stream of orange and blue flame shot forth. Flames began to eat away at the fabric skin, faster and faster, until in minutes all that remained was the steel skeleton enveloped in an inferno of fire. A gondola broke loose and fell slowly to the ground.

Fascinated, Edward was slow to realize his danger. Pushed by the wind, the fiery holocaust was falling directly toward his plane. At the last moment Edward banked violently to avoid the pyre that plunged by barely a hundred feet away with a roaring and a tremendous wave of heat, as if a furnace door had been flung open. Then he was clear except for a few flaming fragments that floated by. The burning mass plunged downward and crashed somewhere between Lambeth and the Thames River near the Tower. Ten miles away, speeding for home with his fuel tank almost empty, Edward could still look back and see the fire in the distance.

He wondered how many men a Zeppelin carried—thirty, forty? How many men had he killed that night? Now that the danger was over, the reaction set in and his whole body shook uncontrollably.

"It was a huge Chinese lantern," Edward said in a wondering tone, "shining brightly in the darkness above me. Then it just broke apart, flames everywhere, until nothing was left but steel girders wrapped in a ball of fire."

Major Morgan poured a stiff drink of brandy into a glass and handed it without a word to the exhausted Edward. As soon as the victorious B.E. had landed, it had been surrounded by a jubilant mob of pilots, mechanics, and ground crew. They had lifted Edward from the cockpit and carried him triumphantly on their shoulders, singing and cheering. A telephone call from RFC headquarters had reported the successful attack on the Zeppelin. There had been only one plane still in the air at that time, so there was no doubt as to the identity of the pilot. They had swarmed all over the plane as soon as it had taxied up to the hangar line, pounding Edward on the back and shaking his hand. Someone even called for "three cheers for Lieutenant Burton." After months of frustration the squadron's first victory was heady stuff.

The major had taken one look at Edward's tense face as he was being carried on the shoulders of two burly mechanics and had sharply ordered a halt to the demonstration. He hurried the shivering young pilot into his office and locked the door. Then, without a word, he went to his cabinet and grabbed a bottle of brandy. He had seen that look before on the faces of men when they had been too long at the front.

"Drink that, Burton," the major ordered.

Edward swallowed the burning liquid in one gulp, coughed, and began his report. Slumped in a chair, he tried to be nonchalant about the attack, but his voice kept breaking and he fingered his helmet and goggles nervously. Once he wiped his face with his white scarf, then stared unseeing at the oil and perspiration stains. When he came to the moment the Zeppelin had caught fire, he had to stop and get control of himself. Major Morgan sat behind his desk and listened without interrupting.

"It almost fell on me," Edward continued. "I was so paralyzed by what was happening I didn't realize how close it was. It was pure luck that I got out of the way in time. It went down somewhere near the river south of Tower Bridge. God only knows what it landed on."

The telephone rang shrilly. Major Morgan picked it up and spoke quietly into it. Edward could hear a loud, enthusiastic voice on the other end, but his numbed mind could not grasp the words. A grimace of distaste curled Morgan's lips as he listened, and he tapped his fingers impatiently on the desk as the voice went on and on. Finally he ended the conversation with a curt "Yes sir, I understand. Yes, I have Lieutenant Burton right now. Tomorrow at ten? Very good. Goodbye, sir." He put the telephone down abruptly.

"I'm sorry, Burton, but it looks like the ordeal isn't over yet. That was General Masterman, the high muckety-muck in charge of RFC relations with the government. You probably know what an uproar there has been in the press these last months about our failure to stop these Zeppelin raids. The public has been upset too, and last week there was a question raised in the House of Commons about the inefficiency of our air raid defenses. Well, your victory tonight has changed all of that. It seems that nearly a million Londoners saw that Zeppelin come down in flames and are cheering the pilot. The general, of course, sees this as a wonderful opportunity to turn public opinion in our favor and win support in the Commons for more planes and men."

The major paused and fiddled with some papers on his desk. It was clear that he was embarrassed by what he had to say. "The general has arranged a press conference tomorrow at ten at the War Office. There'll be newspapermen and photographers there, all eager to interview the man who brought down the first Zeppelin. Sorry about this, but it's orders."

Edward stared at the floor. "Do you mean that I'm to be put on display to please the public?"

"Nothing like that," Morgan said sharply, "just tell them what happened. The general will take care of the rest." He looked at the exhausted young pilot on the other side of the desk and knew that this whole business was going to turn out badly. Burton was not the sort of man who would stand for being lionized for doing his duty—and a distasteful duty at that. Still, it was orders and they were both soldiers. Time to remind Burton of that.

"Civilian morale is a very important factor in this war," the major said. "The supply of guns and planes depends on public support. Keep that in mind tomorrow. Now get some rest. You leave at 8:30 A.M. for London. That's all."

Edward rose wearily from the chair and saluted.

At the door he turned and asked, "Where did the Zeppelin come down?"

"We were lucky there. It fell in a wooded area behind a factory east of Southwark. No one on the ground was hurt, and the fire it started was quickly put out."

"Any survivors?" Edward knew the answer even before he asked, but there was some aching need to hear it.

"No, Burton, there were no survivors."

Edward nodded unhappily. He opened the door and went out.

At forty-one, General Masterman was young for a brigadier. But since the beginning of the war his rise had been meteoric. A graduate of the military college at Sandhurst, he had served with distinction in the Boer War on the staff of the commander in chief. He had come back from South Africa a captain posted to the War Office, the perfect spot for an ambitious junior officer. Five years before, his delicate political antennae had quivered when the formation of the new Royal Flying Corps was proposed. Promotion would be more rapid in a brand-new service than in the hierarchy-ridden traditional army, but Major Masterman had no thought of qualifying as a military pilot. The idea of risking his neck and his career in smelly flying machines was ridiculous to him. By flattery and first-class staff work he made himself indispensable to the new commander of the RFC, a former cavalry officer totally

lost among the fliers and machines. The outbreak
of the war in 1914 had brought opportunity without limit as the RFC was expanded to meet the
demands of air combat on the Western Front.
Promotion followed, and in 1916 Masterman put
on the red tabs of a brigadier general, in charge
of government and public relations.

His job was to sell the members of Parliament
and the man in the street on the vital role of the
RFC in this war—not an easy task as losses
mounted and requests for money increased. The
outcry against the Zeppelin raids had been particularly painful, since it was impossible to hide
the civilian deaths as he had been able to minimize
the terrible casualties among the pilots in the
field. But today he was exuberant as he sat smiling
behind his desk, looking proudly at the handsome
young pilot standing at attention in front of him.
Lieutenant Edward Burton was the answer to
all his problems—and just in time, thank God.
What a marvelous coup this was—a young, good-
looking, gallant pilot who shoots down a Zeppelin
in front of a million spectators. Patriotic, too—
went out in 1914 as a mechanic. Seven victories
in the air; three medals, including the Military
Cross; twice mentioned in dispatches. Have to
soft-pedal that unfortunate business about his
medical history.

"At ease, Lieutenant," Brigadier Masterman said
with a satisfied smile. What a public hero this boy
will make! This publicity should shut the mouths
of all those carpers in the House of Commons who

kept asking embarrassing questions about our losses in France.

Edward came to parade rest, his eyes fixed on the immaculately dressed brigadier, whose leather and buttons gleamed. Edward knew he had an orderly to take care of those things, but he still felt positively shabby in comparison. Edward stared across the desk and waited.

"Now about this conference," Masterman said. "I'll have an opening statement"—To make certain that *your* name appears prominently in the news accounts, Edward thought—"then you'll describe your gallant attack on the Zeppelin, not forgetting how you lightened your plane to get up there. You might mention your American father for the Yank correspondents present—they'll go for that. And, oh yes, say something about how you were eager to return to your brave comrades in France but you recognized how vital was the protection of our civilians against these murderous air raids. Do you have all that?"

Edward nodded slowly, not trusting himself to speak. "Good," the brigadier continued, "then we can go."

They left the office and walked down the wide corridor. Junior officers stood respectfully to one side, and a dozen doors opened to allow the occupants a glimpse of "the man who shot down a Zeppelin." Edward stared straight ahead, hating every minute of it, but Masterman smiled amiably at everyone, showing off his publicity prize. An elderly colonel stepped forward suddenly and without a word shook Edward's hand solemnly. Touched by the unexpected accolade, the young pilot tried to smile and say something modest, but the words choked him. It was all so false and ostentatious. "You'll enjoy this," Masterman breathed in his ear as they entered the conference room. Poker-faced, Edward did not acknowledge the remark. His head was pounding and he felt disgusted.

The large wood-paneled room was crowded with a mob of chattering reporters and photographers, all crowding forward toward the long oak table at the back. A blue haze from the smoke of cigarettes, cigars, and pipes hung over the crowd as Edward and General Masterman pushed their way through, accompanied by a light patter of applause. Even to the cynical newspaper people the tall young lieutenant looked like a hero. "That face in the evening papers will break a lot of shopgirls' hearts," one reporter whispered to his cameraman.

Behind the table, Edward at his side, Masterman raised a hand and waited confidently for silence. The hum of conversation died.

"Gentlemen," the brigadier said solemnly, "thank you for coming here today. I know that you are all anxious to meet and speak to the hero of yesterday's downing of the Zeppelin"—Edward cringed at the praise—"but I thought it best to start with a short summary of Lieutenant Burton's outstanding service in the Royal Flying Corps. He's much too modest to speak of his many feats of valor himself, so let me do it so that you may inform your readers of what a gallant young man stands next to me today."

Masterman then proceeded to describe how Edward had enlisted on the first day of the war as a mechanic in the RFC since he was too young for pilot training. The clipped, educated voice went on and on . . . "first spotted the Germans moving on Mons . . . shot down an enemy plane with one of the first machine guns mounted in an airplane . . . when he was of age, trained as a fighter pilot . . . seven victories over enemy planes in France . . . wounded and hospitalized, returned to England on convalescent leave. Although he pleaded to be returned to his squadron in France, the pressing need for experienced fliers to protect the civilian population from Zeppelin raids led to his assignment to the Home Defence Wing. . . . His brilliant service in France has now been topped by his exploit in shooting down a Zeppelin single-handed."

As Masterman stopped for breath a reporter quickly asked, "Lieutenant, exactly how old are you?" The brigadier glared at the brash newspaperman but remained silent.

"I'll be nineteen on the twelfth of this month." Edward's voice was low and there were several shouts of "louder" from the back of the room.

"I notice that you are wearing the shoulder badge of the Royal *Canadian* Flying Corps. Isn't that unusual?" Masterman looked flustered, but Edward grinned and said, "There was some question about my citizenship since my mother is English and my father is American. When I applied for pilot training, this question came up and it was decided that it was best resolved by my joining the Canadians, who were allowed to recruit Americans." The brigadier sighed in relief and shot a grateful glance at Edward.

"Your father's name and address, please, Lieutenant?" The question came from a tall, long-nosed reporter directly in front of the table.

Startled, Edward blurted, "His name is Thomas Burton and he lives at 921 Pine Street, Philadelphia, Pennsylvania. He is a stockbroker."

The man who had asked the question grinned and waved his pencil happily. "The correspondent of the *Philadelphia Public Ledger* thanks you, Lieutenant, for a great story-line."

"As does the correspondent of *The Toronto Star*," someone shouted. "Remember to mention, Yank, that he's fighting with the RCFC!"

There was a burst of laughter at this exchange, and Masterman smiled happily. It was going splendidly after an impertinent question, which Burton had handled beautifully. *Amazing young fellow—great poise and quickness of mind. Might be a spot for him in the War Office after this buildup.*

Several questions on the attack on the Zeppelin came next, and Edward answered them easily and modestly, refusing to wrap himself in the hero's mantle that Masterman had prepared for him. It had been his duty, the young pilot insisted, to destroy enemy dirigibles, and he had done that and no more. He had been lucky to have found the Zeppelin in the dark just before his fuel ran out.

Flashes of light filled the room as the photographers took pictures with the help of exploding magnesium powder. Edward felt the brigadier moving slightly closer to make certain that he was included. Then he saw the reporters crowded in front of the table give way and allow a short, balding, red-faced man of about fifty to come forward. Edward was surprised at the respect that such an unimposing figure obviously commanded. Who was he?

The dumpy little man answered the question himself. "Remington, Lieutenant, of *The Times*. Might I ask a few questions?"

Edward nodded and saw Masterman stiffen. The name was a famous one, the military expert of *The Times*, a man who had sent his dispatches home from a hundred battlefields, always accurate, always concise, always first. Already in this war he had exposed the shortcomings of the military establishment a dozen times: the shell shortages in the early days, the futile attacks against barbed wire and machine guns by waves of men who were mowed down without a chance; and the criminal stupidity of senior officers who did not even inspect the ground over which they ordered men to advance. Henry Remington was hated more in the War Office than the enemy himself.

"Of course, Mr. Remington," Edward said politely, enjoying the brigadier's nervousness.

The Times's military correspondent consulted a notebook. "Is it true, Lieutenant, that you were invalided home last July because of a nervous breakdown brought on by the stress of combat flying?"

There was a dismayed murmur in the room and a few protests at the question. Edward held up his hand for silence. "Yes, Mr. Remington," he said quietly, "that is exactly right. After twenty-two months in France I had given all I had to give. When I lost my best friend in a burning plane, I broke. When they lifted me out of the cockpit of my plane, I was talking gibberish."

The room was dead silent now as Edward paused. "Obviously you can't trust a man in that condition in a combat situation, so they sent me back to England and later made me a flying instructor. But I complained so much that they sent me to a Home Defence unit to shut me up."

Masterman started to interrupt, but Remington was too quick for him. "Complained about what, Lieutenant?" Pencils were scribbling rapidly over the writing pads as the other reporters took down this unexpected twist in the interview.

Edward felt the blood rush to his face. He had been a soldier long enough to resent the way the war was pictured in the newspapers. It was more than just newspaper copy, a chance to titillate readers with tales of bloody battles. Still, he felt very strongly about the shortcomings of pilot training, and the newspapers were very influential.

"Complained about sending untrained men, green fliers who don't know the first thing about air combat, out to face German aces in France. Men with less than ten hours' solo are being sacrificed because of the mistakes made here in this building. Blundering senior officers who should have been retired before the war are making decisions about a new type of warfare that they cannot conceivably understand. And not only in France— right here, too. To fight Zeppelins they have given us an out-of-date plane that can't even reach the altitude that the Zeppelins fly at. And incendiary rounds in our guns that are useless. Madness, that's what it is, sheer stupidity and madness. If it goes on, we'll lose this war."

Suddenly Edward was aware that Masterman was gone from his side and that the reporters were staring at him strangely. He wiped his face with his hand, started to apologize, then was silent. Apologize for what?

Remington pursed his lips thoughtfully and said, "Thank you, Lieutenant Burton. In my opinion, what you have just said took more courage than attacking that Zeppelin. Your superiors won't thank you for it, but I do. You are a very brave young man."

As the reporters and photographers filed silently from the room a smartly dressed captain with the red staff brassard on his arm hurried into the room. When the last reporter was gone, he walked up to the table and grinned at Edward. "Must have been quite a news conference, Burton. Not exactly what General Masterman had in mind. I thought he was going to explode. Came storming into General Wallace's office demanding your immediate execution. Well, he wasn't exactly organizing a firing squad—not yet—but right now he's looking for the farthest and most dismal post in the RFC for you. China, I think. Do you speak Chinese, Burton? No? Too bad. Oh well, maybe it will only be some pesthole in Mesopotamia, sand, flies, all sorts of evil diseases."

The captain was clearly enjoying Masterman's defeat. Edward only half listened, trying to swallow the lump in his throat. Breathing deeply, he threw back his shoulders and walked around the table, and headed for the door.

"Oh, one moment, Burton, if you please," the captain said with a knowing smile. "Sorry, but you're under close arrest. I'm to escort you forthwith back to Fawkes Green. Orders of General Wallace, with no little assistance from the late king of press relations."

There was a staff car waiting for them in Whitehall, an armed guard in the front seat next to the driver. General Masterman was taking no chances that Edward might talk again to civilians.

4

Edward's diary for January 12, 1917:

Today is my nineteenth birthday and my ninth day of close arrest. Major Morgan stopped in to cheer me up. He told me that the War Office is having a hard time deciding what to do with me. The furore over the sensational newspaper reports has still not died down. *The Times* had the most sober and thoughtful article—trust Remington for that—but it still blistered the War Office for its inefficiency. When all the questions raised in the House of Commons are answered, I'll be on a ship to some Godforsaken spot far from here. I hope it is soon. This room is more and more like a jail.

"Close arrest" means that he was relieved of all duties and confined to his quarters except for

meals, to which he was escorted by an armed officer. The other pilots treated the whole business
as a big joke and a great lark. The news of the
uproar over the press conference had been greeted
with loud laughter, for there was no love lost between the haughty top brass on the staff and the
men who did the flying. Edward was a hero, and in
the mess hall he was elaborately waited on by his
fellow fliers. Even the officer-escort refused to take
his duties seriously, often leaving Edward free to
wander around the airfield unattended. It was
understood that Edward would not try to escape.

But not flying and not hearing from Ann made
his confinement agonizing. He knew that she had
seen the newspapers and must be aware that he
was in serious trouble, but there was no word
from her. By now he was too proud to keep
telephoning.

On the twelfth day, Major Morgan sent for him
and, grim-faced, handed him his orders. Lieutenant Edward Burton was to report at once to the
RFC depot at Farnborough. There he was to pick
up a plane and ferry it to France. Further orders
would be given him at the depot. By order of General Henderson, etc., etc.

"Does this mean that I'm assigned to ferry duty,
sir?" Edward asked. Resigned to a court-martial
for "conduct unbecoming an officer and a gentle-
man," he was bewildered by being ordered to a
post usually given pilots of much less experience.

Morgan shook his head. "It doesn't say that,
Burton. I think they're sending you to an operational squadron at the front. Only they don't want

to put it in black and white where anyone can see it, so it will be given to you verbally at Farnborough. Sorry, but I think they're getting rid of a troublesome officer by sending him back to get himself killed at the front."

Well, Edward thought, this is what I asked for back at the flying school, but I never thought it would come because the War Office wanted me dead.

Late that afternoon a boisterous crowd of pilots and ground officers gathered around a dusty staff car to give Edward a squadron farewell. There were speeches extolling his courage—"Led the attack on the entrenched forces in the War Office"—rounds of cheers, and, finally, handshakes and embarrassed mumbles. The major had said his good-byes earlier and had discreetly absented himself so that he would not have to reprimand anyone for outrageous remarks about certain superior officers. Better not to hear them in the first place.

The burly Irish corporal-driver skirted London to the west while keeping up a cheerful line of chatter. Edward barely heard him. Slumped in his seat, he stared out at the snow-filled fields and shivering towns, his mind grappling with the question of where they would send him. With all his heart he wanted to go back to his friends in Number Twenty-four Squadron: Sergeant Foley, "Doggo" Wooley, even Captain Fortescue, who had first taught him to fly. That seemed a long time ago, but it was only three years since he was a schoolboy learning how to fly straight and level in

Captain Fortescue's Blériot. Today he was a military aviator in disgrace and Fortescue a squadron commander.

The depot at Farnborough was a large mass of red-brick buildings, hangars, and scattered repair, assembly, and test sheds. As he got out of the staff car in front of the headquarters building and acknowledged the smart salute of the sentries, Edward could see a line of new fighter planes wing tip to wing tip on the tarmac. It was a sight to take the breath from a seasoned pilot. There were almost fifty planes in a row—more aircraft than he had ever seen together in one place before—not to mention the reconnaissance, bomber, and even training planes that he could see on the wide airfield.

The adjutant read his orders and tried to pretend that Edward's assignment was purely routine. No, there had been no further news about where Lieutenant Burton was being posted. He would be informed as soon as the new orders came in. In the meantime he was to be checked out on one of the new fighters—the Sopwith Camel—and was to be ready in five days to fly it to France. That was all.

Edward understood the adjutant's nervousness and did not take offense at his curtness. He knew that he was an embarrassment. Any pilot who had incurred the wrath of the top brass was bound to be. But he noticed that the adjutant, a husky blond captain, was wearing pilot's wings and the red and blue ribbon of the Flying Cross, so he was certain of a fair hearing at this post.

"I served with Number Twenty-four Squadron last year," Edward said softly. "I have a lot of friends there. It would be nice to see them again."

The captain shuffled the papers on his desk hurriedly and grunted as Edward continued. "We were together, some of us, with old Number Four back in August '14. Went over together in the first flight." It was said in an offhand way as if it were not important, but Edward watched the adjutant's face carefully.

The captain looked up and grinned. "I get the point, Burton. Always nicer flying with friends. I'll see what can be done, but I can't promise anything. We got a real blast from the War Office about you—'Bolshie troublemaker' was one of the kinder things they called you—but I read the newspaper accounts of that interview too. So I'll do my best. Report to Lieutenant Fellings on the flight line when you're squared away with quarters."

Edward saluted and marched out. As he stepped out of the headquarters building, five of the Sopwith fighters were taxiing out for takeoff. He stood in front of the car and watched with a professional eye until they had roared down the strip and climbed rapidly into the cloudless sky. He noted that one of the planes skidded badly in making a right turn at low altitude. The pilot recovered clumsily and soon the five planes were black dots in the east. Have to watch that, Edward thought. That Camel seems to have a lot of torque in a turn. He got back into the car and was driven to his new home.

Lieutenant Fellings was a small, wiry Cornish-man with a long red scar on his left cheek ("A broken strut gave me a shave when I crashed six months ago"). It was only later that Edward learned that the peppery little instructor had taken on four Fokkers single-handedly and had shot down two before having his controls riddled. It was a miracle that he had survived the crash in no-man's-land and the two operations on his leg that followed. He walked with a slight limp as he circled the Camel, explaining its fine points to the attentive Burton.

"A lovely plane, Burton, absolutely a beauty. You'll love it. It has everything: speed of a hundred twenty-five miles per hour at ground level; climbs to ten thousand feet in just over ten minutes; a ceiling of twenty-one thousand feet; quick to turn and highly maneuverable. She'll outfight anything the Jerries have today. Look at those twin Vickers, those lovely lines." It was clear that the man adored the new plane. It was a passion that Edward well understood, that special feeling of a flier for his airplane. The crusader must have had the same feeling for his war steed. But Edward was cautious—any warhorse could be touchy and throw its rider at the wrong time.

At the front of the Camel, Edward pointed up to the engine. "I've never flown a rotary-engine plane before. Isn't there a lot of torque on the turns?"

Fellings frowned. "Oh, yes, it takes a bit of getting used to, but once you master it, you'll find it a big help in whipping around when there's a Jerry on your tail. She's so sensitive that all you have to do is think of turning and she's in a bank."

Edward looked doubtfully at the exposed engine. Unlike the conventional engine, in which the propeller was attached to the crankshaft and the rest of the engine fixed, the Clerget rotary had a fixed crankshaft and the cylinders rotated about it, carrying the propeller with it ("better air cooling," Fellings explained).

The instructor went step by step through the takeoff and landing procedure. "Watch the torque on the turns. The nose will drop in a right turn and rise in a left one. Correct quickly or you'll find yourself in a bloody spin. Cruise at eighty-five and keep up your flying speed at all times. Make your approach at seventy and just fly her all the way down to flareout. She lands beautifully, but keep her straight on the landing roll. The landing gear is rather close together, and she'll ground-loop if you let her get away from you."

Edward climbed into the cockpit and looked around. The instruments all looked familiar, but something was missing. "Where's the throttle?" he asked in a puzzled tone. Fellings laughed and shook his head. "No throttle on a rotary, old boy," he explained. "They always run at full throttle. You come down by interrupting the ignition by flipping this button on the control stick. Now here's the start-up procedure." The instructor explained the pilot's role when the engine was being cranked and pulled through. "Just stay on the brakes. This is a very reliable engine, so don't worry. Taxi her around the field a few times and get the feel of her on the ground."

Fellings stepped down from the wing and signaled to a mechanic. After the propeller was turned twice to suck fuel into the cylinders, the mechanic looked inquiringly at Edward. The young pilot made a last check of the instrument panel, tightened his safety belt, and gave the thumb-up signal. Ready to start.

Firmly grasping one blade of the propeller, the grease monkey raised his right leg and pulled the blade vigorously through its arc. After a slight sputter the engine roared into full life. Edward checked his brakes nervously as the plane strained forward. He flipped the switch as he had been warned to do. ("Otherwise the petrol piles up in the cylinders and when she sparks—boom!") That "boom!" had sounded ominous indeed.

Releasing the brakes at a signal from the mechanic, Edward began to taxi across the field. The Camel kept accelerating, and he had to touch the brakes softly to keep it from running away. He had never sat in a plane so eager to fly. Turning from side to side to give himself a clear view of possible obstacles ahead, Edward taxied the plane to the far end of the airfield and lined it up on the takeoff strip into the light wind.

Very well, Mr. Sopwith, he thought, if you're so eager to take to the air, let's go and see what you can do.

Making certain that there was no plane on a landing approach, Edward let the Camel pick up speed down the runway. It accelerated rapidly, as he had expected, and with the slightest back pressure on the control stick broke ground contact and climbed. The torque was severe, but Edward held left rudder firmly until he had enough flying speed so that the offset in the vertical stabilizer took effect. After that it was a marvelous flight. Fellings was right. The Camel was a Thoroughbred among planes.

He climbed to five thousand feet and put the plane through its paces: steep turns, loops, an Immelmann (which was a half-loop followed by a half-roll), steep dives—the whole catalogue of acrobatics that he had learned as a fighter pilot on the Western Front. It was exhilarating to throw an airplane around in the sky, and it had been a long time since Edward had known the wild freedom of flying without restraint. He knew that he was rusty, but his loops and Immelmanns were clean. Five hours of familiarization flying and he would master the Sopwith Camel.

Blipping the engine, he dropped down swiftly and approached the field. He could see Fellings and the mechanic standing on the tarmac watching him, so he concentrated on making a good landing. All the way around the pattern circuit he held his airspeed closely, turned shallowly on the final approach, held the center line of the runway, and flared out at just the right time. The Camel floated as if reluctant to leave the air, then touched down and rumbled across the grassy strip. As the plane slowed, Edward used the brakes easily to taxi up to the hangar line. He switched off the engine and sat back satisfied as the propeller arc disappeared into slowly rotating blades, which then stopped.

Fellings walked up to the cockpit and said, "Well?" Edward grinned happily. "A beauty. The very finest I've ever flown." He climbed down from the cockpit and shook Fellings's hand in appreciation. The instructor laughed and slapped him on the back. Between fliers nothing more needed to be said, and Fellings did not mention that Edward had taken off without permission.

The next morning when Edward awoke, the airfield was covered with a light fog. After a hasty breakfast he hurried down to the hangar to wait impatiently until the sun had burned off the last wisps of fog. Then he got into the plane and took off. The mechanics smiled at his eagerness, but Fellings was pleased and authorized as many hours as Edward thought he would need in the new plane.

For three days, Edward spent every spare minute flying, testing the Camel and himself. It was essential to get the "feel" of a new plane, to master the thousand and one little tricks that finally molded the plane and its pilot into one. A doctor at the flying school had told him that it was a matter of training deep muscle responses, not the "seat of the pants" feelings that pilots talked of. Edward was not certain exactly what the doctor meant, but after a few hours he found he knew the speed of the plane without looking at the gauge. He could tell when the Camel wanted to fly and when it just wanted to wallow about on the edge of a stall. Then he would coax it back to normal flight.

Coming back to the airfield on the third day, Edward glanced out of the cockpit as he was approaching the end of the runway at low altitude. Three hundred feet below, sitting in a lounge chair in a formal garden, an elderly lady wrapped in an old-fashioned cloak looked up from under her parasol and waved a handkerchief gaily. Edward blipped the engine in acknowledgment and waved back.

"Do you know who lives over there?" he later asked Fellings, pointing to the large house at the southern end of the field. "There's a nice old lady in the garden who seems to like fliers."

The instructor signed Edward's flight record, hiding a mischievous grin. "Do you mean the Empress Eugénie?"

"My God," Edward blurted. "An empress?"

"A real one, old man. Wife of the French Emperor Napoleon the Third. Poor dear, she fled with him after the defeat by the Prussians in 1870 and has lived here ever since. The Emperor died in '73, and their only child, the Prince Imperial, was cut down by Zulu spears five years later. She's all alone now. Yes, she is fond of the fliers and fonder still of what we're doing to those awful 'Prussians.' "

"She must be very old."

"Oh yes, ninety, ninety-one, something like that. It's hard to imagine, isn't it, but as a child she knew Wellington and Talleyrand. She's a marvelous woman. On her birthday every year the C.O.

leads all the officers to her house to pay their respects. Last time she said that she hoped to live long enough to see all 'Prussians' smashed.'"

Edward stared across at the red-roofed mansion. No one he knew at the front felt that way about the Jerries, who were just another bunch of men caught up in this ruthless war. Yes, they shot each other out of the sky, but only because it was their duty. But he had heard that the French pilots hated like that. Perhaps they had not forgotten 1870 either.

Ten days after his arrival at Farnborough, Edward was called to the adjutant's office and handed new orders. To his vast relief he saw that he was to take a new Camel to Number Twenty-four Squadron at Saint-Omer and report to the commanding officer for duty. He started to thank the adjutant, but the captain waved his hand to stop the words. "Pure chance, Burton. No need for thanks. Of course, the orders from the War Office said you were to be sent to Egypt, but that shipment has been delayed and we have an urgent request from RFC headquarters in France for pilots. Can't have you sitting around the depot waiting for a transport ship when you're needed in France, can we? Anyway, I cleared it with the C.O. and he agreed. You leave as soon as the weather clears"—a winter gale had raged for the last two days—"and we hope to have you safe in France—if you'll forgive the unfortunate phrasing—before the top brass realize that you have escaped banishment to the desert."

The storm lasted another two days, and Edward paced his room, waiting. They had given him a Camel fresh from the factory, sparkling in its new paint, its fabric unspotted by oil, and its machine guns still not fired. A dozen times a day Edward fought his way against the icy wind and rain to the hangar to run his hand lovingly over the shiny wings and fuselage. It was such a beautiful thing. He was impatient to get it into the air where it belonged.

January 26 dawned bright, clear, and cold. After last-minute instructions from the adjutant and a firm handshake from the C.O., Edward ordered the plane pushed out to the flight line and warmed up. Satisfied that all was in order, he climbed into the cockpit, made his final checks, waved good-bye to the pilots and men gathered to watch, and began his taxiing to the runway. Three minutes later he was airborne, climbing out over the formal garden at the end of the field. The Empress was undoubtedly fast asleep, dreaming of victory over the "Prussians." Edward rocked his wings in salute to a brave old woman, then set his course for the Channel.

An hour later the Camel crossed the Channel coast south of Dover at a height of five thousand feet. It was a glorious day for flying—high clouds, unlimited visibility, and a strong tail wind. Edward looked down at the sparkling water of the Channel and saw the tiny steamers coming and going, carrying reinforcements to the troops in France and bringing home the wounded and the men on leave. In the north a destroyer cruised to and fro looking for German submarines. It was a peaceful scene from this altitude, but Edward knew it was different on the ships below.

As soon as he was clear of the ships, Edward fired his guns for their first test. They chattered loudly, and the tracers leaped out and curved down to the sea. The noise brought back memories, uneasy recollections of dogfights, planes twisting over the sky. Edward felt a tremor in his right hand—the old anxiety? Well, he had asked to be sent back. He hoped that he would still be able to face the stress of aerial combat. He whispered a fervent prayer that he would not let his friends down.

Calais. A sandy beach with the dark town off to his right. Everything looked old and tired, even the fields. The English landscape had been green where the snow had melted, but here everything seemed to be in mourning, wrapped in a white shroud. The houses and barns were unkempt, badly in need of paint; the fields were deserted, for the men were off with the armies, and the women and children were trying to manage alone. Two and a half years of war and already the land looked defeated.

The course to Saint-Omer required a right turn after Calais, but Edward hesitated and looked off to the left. The front was there, Ypres, the old fighting ground, which everyone called "Wipers." He felt an irresistible urge to fly over and see it again. He checked the fuel gauge—there was enough for a side trip, but not enough to loiter once he got there. The Camel banked left and sped off to the northeast. Foolish, Edward told himself, but I want just one look.

Soon the terrain below began to change. Filled-in shell holes, burnt-out farmhouses, the ugly white scars of deserted trenches twisting across old battlefields. The debris of war, Edward thought. And from this height you can't see the graves—but they're there.

Broken clouds appeared ahead, and Edward climbed to get above them. They were widely scattered but Edward welcomed the chance to leave the sight of the tortured landscape. It was cleaner up above.

He had just passed over the ruins of Poperinge, a town of roofless houses and rubble-choked streets, when a sudden movement caught his eye. Off to his left and several thousand feet above him a dozen black wasps were twisting and turning. They were ten miles away, but Edward knew instantly what it was: a dogfight! Without thinking about his critical fuel supply, Edward pulled back on the control stick and began a climb to the combat.

As the Camel approached, the black dots grew wings, and Edward began to distinguish colors. Four khaki Bristol Scouts were fighting desperately against seven gaudily painted German Albatros D-IIIs. Even as he watched, Edward saw an oily plume of black smoke envelop one of the English fighters. It fell off on a wing and twisted down, tongues of red flame licking at the fuselage. Three against seven—the odds were hopelessly against the British.

At maximum range Edward opened fire, hoping
to distract some of the German attackers. His
tracers fell short but they must have been spotted,
for two Albatroses turned away from their cornered victim to face the new threat. Edward
turned steeply, selected a target, and fired three
short bursts. Bits of fabric exploded from the
enemy's yellow tail, and the Jerry hastily spun
away out of range.

Now it was a wild melee. The sky was filled
with madly cavorting planes, twisting, diving,
turning. Above the roar of his own engine, Edward
could hear the mechanical hammering of machine guns. Colored tracers leaped out of Vickers
and Spandau guns and traced bright lines through
space. It was every man for himself, and the devil
would certainly take the hindmost. His throat dry,
his stomach in a tight knot, Edward threw himself
into the uneven combat, calling on all his skill
and experience to find the slight edge that meant
survival.

The Camel sliced down to help one Bristol
Scout that was slowly losing its fight with three
enemy planes. They had it boxed in, and every
time it tried to break out of the trap a burst of
machine gun fire drove it back. It would be over
soon unless the pilot found help. Edward aimed
carefully at the closest Albatros and fired. Before
the German pilot could turn, the tracers ripped
through his cockpit and raised little puffs of dust
from his black flying jacket. As if to protest the
intrusion, the enemy flier rose in his seat, half

turned, and raised a gloved hand weakly. Then he slumped back and the Albatros stalled and fell into a spin. Edward did not watch it go down. There was no time to savor victory.

Startled, the other two enemy fighters banked sharply, forgetting their prey. At that moment the Bristol scout half-looped with great skill and riddled the belly of one of his tormentors. One of his rounds tore open the fuel tank and sent raw petrol gushing out onto the hot exhaust pipes. In an instant the Albatros was a flaming cloud from which the familiar oily smoke and bits of fabric cascaded. Four against five—the odds were much better now.

So violent had been Edward's attack, and so sudden his appearance, that the enemy pilots hesitated and looked around anxiously for the other British planes that they were certain would be diving down on them. Surely no single plane would intrude so foolishly. The Albatroses reformed and circled at a distance, ready either to return to the attack or to flee.

At that instant the Bristol Scout that Edward had aided rocked its wings and started to dive steeply for the safety of the Allied lines. Edward waited, flying top cover, until the other two British fighters had followed their leader down out of range. When the German pilots saw their prey escaping, they turned to finish off the arrogant Britisher who was defying them.

Edward flung his plane at the approaching Albatroses, fired a burst at long range to make them disperse, then rolled his Camel on its back and split-essed out into a vertical dive. It was a dangerous maneuver in a new plane, one whose limits he did not know, but he had confidence in the sturdy Sopwith. By the time the Germans had turned to follow, he was flying low over the trenches on the tails of the three Bristols. He encountered first some erratic rifle fire from the German troops, then white faces and waving helmets as he sped over the friendly positions. He looked back and saw the frustrated enemy fighters flying north, giving up the chase.

One of the Bristol Scouts dropped back and took up a position off the Camel's left wing. Edward waved, but the other pilot only stared, refusing to return the greeting. Red streamers flowed from the struts of the Scout—a squadron commander, Edward thought, and an unfriendly clod, too. I won't get much thanks from that one.

They flew south for fifteen minutes. One of the Bristols was having engine trouble, and the other planes covered him protectively. Edward looked for landmarks. His fuel was very low, and he would not have time for a long search for the airfield at Saint-Omer. He spotted the snow-covered ruins of Hazebrouck, then the blue thread of the Aa River. A single-track railroad appeared under his right wing and he turned to follow it into Saint-Omer. Immediately the other three planes turned with him. Puzzled, Edward stared at them. Were they low on fuel and going into Saint-Omer to refuel? The only squadron markings on the

Bristols was a large white "D" on the khaki fuse-lage. That meant nothing to Edward, so he shrugged his shoulders and began searching for the airfield southwest of the town. The needle on the fuel gauge was hovering about empty.

He found the field on his first pass, blipped the engine, and fishtailed down to a bumpy landing. The Bristols circled the field as prescribed by regu-lations, then came in one by one. As they taxied up to the flight line, Edward was waiting to greet them. Behind him a crowd of pilots and mechanics was admiring the Sopwith Camel.

The squadron commander's plane taxied up and stopped. From the cockpit a tall, white-faced man emerged, stepping down gingerly and paus-ing to wipe the oil from his face with his white scarf. He eyed Edward for a moment, then slowly walked over. When he pulled off his helmet and goggles, Edward saw with a start that it was Allen Fortescue, an older, grim-faced, disapproving Fortescue. So it was Number Twenty-four Squad-ron he had helped. . . . Well, it was clear that his C.O. did not intend to thank him for it.

"I might have guessed that it was you, Burton," Major Fortescue said bitterly. "Didn't you realize that we were three miles behind enemy lines. If you had been shot down over there, you would have presented the Jerries with one brand-new Sopwith fighter for their inspection. What the devil were you thinking of, barging into that fight?"

Edward clamped his jaws to cut off the angry

retort that had leaped to his lips. "I was thinking that you were in trouble and that I had better lend a hand," he said. His face was flushed. He knew that the rest of the squadron was nearby listening to the uncalled-for rebuke.

Fortescue shook his head wearily as if to clear it. His voice was hard and unyielding. "In the future, Lieutenant, as long as you are under my command, you will exercise better judgment—and obey orders." His lower lip trembled uncontrollably. The man's cracking up, Edward thought. His nerves are gone.

"Sorry, sir," Edward said quietly. "Actually, I had no orders not to engage in combat, but I'll remember your instructions in the future." *Don't antagonize him. He can't take much more.*

The major peered at him suspiciously as if searching for a taunt in the soft words. Then without another word he pushed his way through the crowd to his office. There was a murmur of sympathy from the pilots and mechanics, but Edward could not be certain for whom it was intended.

"Sir!" The voice behind him rang of the parade ground. Even before he turned Edward knew who it was, and he smiled to greet an old friend.

Sergeant-Major Michael Foley was fiftyish, barrel-chested, balding—a soldier of the old school. In August 1914 he had taken a bewildered young civilian recruit named Edward Burton under his wing and shepherded him through the trying first days in the RFC. Foley was not a sentimental man—thirty-five years in the army ruled that out—but he had watched with pride as Edward had measured up to the hard tasks of the early days of the war. A childless widower, the sergeant-major had looked on the young pilot not as a son—that was too romantic—but as the type of young man he would have liked any son of his to have been. When Edward broke after Ogilvie's death, it was Foley who had visited him in the hospital and comforted him, told him not to feel guilty, that Edward had done his best. The friendship between the two men was very close, made just a little distant by the difference in ranks.

"Hello, Sergeant-Major," Edward said with a smile. "As you can see, the bad penny has returned again. I didn't expect the warm welcome given the Prodigal Son, but I didn't think I'd get strips torn off me either." Fortescue's stinging words still hurt.

Foley nodded. "Very wise of the lieutenant not to stand up to the major right now. He's under a bit of a strain, you see, what with Jerry pushing hard in all sectors, shooting us right out of the air. Responsibility of command, you know—damn hard thing sending green men up in worn-out planes that weren't as good as the enemy's got even when they were new. The major's very, very touchy these days, so if I might be so bold as to advise the lieutenant. . . ."

"Understood, Sergeant-Major," Edward said. "I'll be the perfect subordinate—polite, eager to learn, always on time."

"I wouldn't overdo it, sir," Foley whispered.

"Acting unnatural like that might do you harm. I'll show you your quarters now, sir, if you're ready."

Edward nodded and glanced around the airfield as if to reassure himself that he was back with the squadron.

Yes, he was ready—come what may.

5

The Saint-Omer airfield stood on a wide plateau overlooking the valley of the Aa. Before the war it had been a racetrack, where gentlemen in pearl-gray top hats and ladies in fashionable Paris frocks had cheered on their favorites in the steeplechase. Now only the stables remained to serve as repair sheds for more warlike steeds. Three large canvas-and-wood hangars, a small brick headquarters, a motor park, and a mess hall dotted the western end of the airdome. The officers lived in a rundown mansion behind the mess hall, while the enlisted men had to make do with drafty tents and four-man sheds. In February 1917 the airfield was home for two squadrons: the Twenty-fourth and the Thirty-seventh, a reconnaissance squadron flying the ancient F.E. 2 pusher-type observation planes. Together the two squadrons made up Wing Two of the newly expanded RFC and were responsible for fifty miles of the front lines. It was an impossible task.

In the lounge of the mansion that served as the officers' club, Edward was sitting, talking to his friend Captain Lewis "Doggo" Wooley. There was a crackling fire in the fireplace and half a dozen other pilots were sitting there chatting, reading the week-old newspapers and magazines, or enjoying a post-luncheon drink. The room was warm and filled with the acrid odor of tobacco. Voices were low, for everyone was listening for the distant drone of engines that meant the morning patrol was returning. There was a nagging question in each man's mind: How many did we lose today—and whom?

"Doggo" Wooley was a big, husky Yorkshireman of twenty-five with flaming red hair and a broad RFC mustache. Before the war he had been an engineer working in Sheffield. Fascinated by airplanes, he had joined the RFC Reserve in 1913, received his wings in record time, and had been called to active duty when the war broke out. He had gone to France with the first flight of Number Four Squadron in August 1914, along with a sixteen-year-old private-observer-mechanic named Edward Burton. Doggo was a boisterous, hard-drinking pilot who had gotten his nickname by devising an ingenious maneuver for getting out of tight spots in the air fighting. Whenever he was cornered and outnumbered, he would put his plane into a spin and plunge down as if out of control. At the last minute he would recover and speed away at ground level to safety, leaving the enemy pilots cursing far above. Once he had come back with tree branches stuck in his landing gear.

"You must remember, Edward," Wooley said, "that the Jerries have put their best squadrons opposite us. Unlike the RFC, they put their top fliers in a few squadrons under their leading aces and move them around to the trouble spots. Also, their Albatroses and the new Fokkers are better than anything we can put into the air—faster, more maneuverable, better armed—and you can see why the situation is so hairy. Until we get more Camels, we are fighting a losing battle."

Edward frowned. "It's not as if they outnumbered us."

"No," Wooley admitted. "We have a few more planes than they do in this sector, but their equipment gives them an overwhelming advantage. We're losing three planes to every one that we bring down."

"These Bristol Scouts," Edward said derisively. He had been flying the Bristol for the last three weeks and had found it a big disappointment. The Sopwith Camel he had brought to the squadron had been taken by Major Fortescue—"Rank has its privileges, old man," Wooley had observed— and although new Camels were promised soon, the rest of the squadron was still flying the underpowered, clumsy Scouts, which were long overdue for the junk heap.

"Well," Edward said thoughtfully, "if we can't beat them by numbers or better equipment, we damn well better do it with brains."

Doggo stared at the intense younger man and grunted, "How?"

A phonograph blared out the latest music-hall

tune while Edward thought out his answer. It was an idea he had originally stumbled on more than a year ago when he was flying with Iain Ogilvie and trying to protect him.

"Look, Doggo," he said excitedly, "what is the weakness of a fighter plane?"

"Guns point forward, old boy, can't fire back when the Jerries come down on your tail."

"Exactly. We're always vulnerable to an attack from the rear. Even when you've got an enemy plane in your sights, you always have to keep looking over your shoulder to see if his buddy isn't there with *you* in his sights. Makes it hard to shoot straight."

"So?" Wooley's voice had a puzzled note. All this was obvious.

"So what if you didn't have to worry about your tail. Suppose *your* buddy was back there to make certain that no Jerry bothered you. Then you could concentrate on getting the blighter in front and not have to worry about any Jerries in the rear."

"I say, Edward, that means that only half our planes are fighting. The other half are bumbling around back there just watching. Can't see how cutting our strength in half that way . . ."

Edward shook his head impatiently. "Not just watching. If any Jerry comes down on the front man's tail, his bodyguard is there to drive the danger away. Don't you see, Doggo, it means you don't have to keep looking back all the time. Your tail is always covered. It would be like having a man behind you with a machine gun firing back-

ward . . . a two-seater, only we're doing the same
thing with two one-seaters."

Wooley sipped his drink and thought it over.
The idea was attractive in principle, but was it
practical? "You understand," he finally said, "that
the front man gets all the victories, all the medals
and glory and all that bushwa. Do you think that
many pilots will agree to flying the rear?"

Edward's face was stony. He hated the idea of
glory-hunting when men's lives were at stake. "I
thought the idea was to bring down as many Jerry
planes as possible at the smallest loss to our-
selves. To hell with who gets the victories and the
publicity!"

Doggo held up a hand mockingly as if to ward
off an assault. "Don't shoot, Edward. I agree."
He waved his glass in the direction of headquarters. "But you'll have to get Fortescue's con-
sent to try this, you understand."

And there's the rub, Edward thought bitterly.
His relations with the C.O. had gone downhill
since the first day. Fortescue had alternated between biting comments on Edward's flying, his
dress, and his "damned impertinent attitude." The
other pilots had watched the major castigate a
popular pilot with growing indignation, but they
were helpless to do anything. In more than one
mind was the comforting thought, "Thank God
it's not me." Still, the major's behavior, his hysterical outbursts and contradictory orders, had
led to a lowering of squadron morale that was
alarming. Only yesterday, he had put under close

arrest a pilot who had complained too loudly in the mess about the state of their planes, then had rescinded the order an hour later. It was doubtful that the C.O. would welcome a suggestion on tactics from a subordinate he clearly despised.

How should one approach a man who was tottering on the edge of a nervous breakdown? With a sigh Edward remembered another Fortescue— a tall, smiling, genial man, the very model of a Grenadier Guardsman, the enthusiastic pilot who had first shown the callow schoolboy the wonders of flying. How patient he had been then, guiding Edward through his first uncertain steps toward mastery of the airplane. Now the patient instructor was a bitter, overworked martinet to whom a suggestion on tactics from his first student might appear to be insulting. There was no telling what Fortescue's reaction would be, but it had to be done.

"I'll talk to him tonight," Edward said. "Might catch him in a good mood after dinner." Doggo laughed derisively at the idea and wished him luck.

One of the pilots was standing at the window watching the cloudless sunlit sky for the first sign of the returning patrol. "Do you chaps realize what an upside-down, arse-backward world we live in? Back in England they are enjoying this beautiful cold, clear day and praying for more, and we, well, we pray for rain and snow and low clouds. Anything not to have to fly today or tomorrow. Damned funny, isn't it?"

There was laughter at this sally. Then Wooley held up his hand for silence and said, "Listen."

It was only a distant hum at first, then it grew louder, the droning of engines, like a swarm of bees approaching. The morning flight was coming home.

No one rushed to the door to see how many had returned. Almost indifferently they returned to their reading and their drinks, but someone shut off the phonograph and there was absolute silence in the room. The wind was out of the west, so the landing planes would fly directly over the mansion. As they roared over at low altitude everyone counted silently. Five Bristol Scouts had taken off just after dawn to escort two F.E. 2s on a photographic mission deep in German-occupied France. Seven was the magic number they were praying for, seven engines roaring over them, all home safe.

There were five—then silence. Doggo cleared his throat gruffly and swallowed his drink. "Let's go, Edward. Might as well know the worst."

They rose and went out, followed by a gloomy group of pilots, to find out who had not returned from the morning patrol.

In the mess hall that night the pilots made an obvious attempt to ignore the two empty chairs. By tradition they should have been removed earlier, but the mess orderlies had been thrown into a panic by Fortescue. Claiming he had found a half-washed glass at his place, the C.O. had had all the plates, silverware, and glasses removed and thoroughly cleaned. While the hungry pilots milled around complaining bitterly of the delay, Fortescue inspected the kitchen, giving out punishment tours liberally to the cooks and helpers before allowing dinner to be served.

"He could just have changed his glass," Wooley grumbled. Edward said nothing.

"Well?" Major Fortescue's tone was belligerent and angry. Under the light of the single exposed light bulb over his desk, his skin was an unhealthy yellow. His fingers kept up a nervous tattoo on the arm of his chair as he stared at Edward standing at attention in front of the desk.

Immaculate in his best dress uniform, Edward said, "Sir, I have permission to speak to the commanding officer." He had been careful to go through all the formalities of requesting an interview from the adjutant and had taken great pains with his dress so as not to give the major any excuse to find fault.

Fortescue grunted suspiciously. "Get on with it, Burton. What's this all about?"

Edward explained his idea for breaking the flights into two-plane units, one to attack and the other to protect the attacker's tail. He listed the advantages and the probability of reducing losses —the major twitched at the word—and of increasing the squadron's score of enemy planes brought down. "Of course, sir, the rear man will have to do a nice bit of flying to stay in position through all the acrobatics but . . ."

"Nonsense," the major said, rubbing his jaw with a shaking hand.

"Sir?"

"Complete nonsense. Rubbish. Reduces our fire-power by half, requires a level of flying skill most of our men don't have, and puts the rear man in an untenable dangerous position. The Jerries will knock him down first, then the front man is cold meat. Ridiculous."

Edward kept his voice low and respectful. "If you'll let me continue, sir—"

"No." There was the shrill, hysterical note in the major's voice that warned Edward not to go on. Fortescue was glaring now. Edward fought down the angry words that bubbled in his throat, saluted, and marched out of the office. *My God, our lives are in the hands of that man!*

As he walked out of the headquarters building, Wooley was waiting in the darkness. After one look at Edward's face as he stood in the lighted doorway, the husky redhead took the younger man's arm and led him away. They walked along the hangar lines, saying nothing until they reached the path that ran down the hill to town. The cold air lessened Edward's anger, and by the time they had walked a mile he was almost feeling sorry for the major.

"I don't know how he can go on, Doggo. He looks like a corpse. His hands are always shaking. Yet I can't forget what he was like before the war, when I was a schoolboy and he was teaching me to fly. How I looked up to him, admired him, wanted nothing more than to be just like him. A marvelous flier—which he still is in spite of all his problems—patient, good-humored, yes, even gentle. It tears my guts to see him this way. I don't know why he hates me so."

Wooley kicked a branch off the road. "Not too hard to understand, old man. The rest of us are just names on the operations board to the major. Oh, yes, it hurts when we go down, but he can live with that—being a Guards officer and knowing men are killed in wartime. But you, Edward, he taught you to fly! You wouldn't be here if he hadn't sold you on flying. The poor sod is torn apart every time he sees you, and he's dreading the day you don't come back."

Edward thought over what Wooley had said. Yes, it was probably true that Fortescue felt a special responsibility for Edward's being at the front as a flier, but he must know that even if he had not taught Edward to fly, Edward could not have escaped the war. They were conscripting men in England now, so it would simply have been the trenches instead of the air. No, Doggo was only partly right. It was being in command, giving the orders that sent green men up against German veterans, that was killing the major. Edward was only an extra burden.

"They should send him home," Edward said compassionately. "He's had enough. First the trenches for a year and now over a year of combat flying. There's a limit to what a man can take." And I know that limit, Edward thought.

In front of the mansion they paused for a last look at the night sky. "If Fortescue leaves," Edward said, "the senior flight commander takes over. That's you, Doggo."

Wooley looked aghast at the idea of commanding the squadron. "In that case, old boy, I shall pray nightly for Major Fortescue's continued good health. No giving orders for me if I can avoid it. Couldn't take that for too long."

Edward laughed at the melancholy look on his friend's face. Then Doggo grinned as a happy thought struck him. "Don't laugh. If it happened, my first order will be to make you Red Flight leader. Nothing like sharing the burden of command, old boy."

The casual remark stunned Edward. It had never occurred to him that if the war and he both lasted long enough, it was inevitable that he should command at least a flight. It was a frightening thought. How would he stand up to the pressure that had broken a man like Allen Fortescue— a professional soldier?

The war went on. Doggo's younger brother, a lieutenant in the Middlesex Rifles, arrived one day on a pass from the trenches. He told them quietly, as if it were the most natural thing in the world, that over a thousand men were being killed or wounded on a "normal" day at the front. When he left, he shook Doggo's hand and said good-bye in a regretful voice that made Edward uneasy. *He doesn't expect to see him again. The odds are all against it.* After seeing his brother off, Doggo went to his room, locked the door, and got drunk.

The next morning was cold and clear with a strong breeze from the north. Red Flight was to escort three F.E. 2s on a bombing run over the German trenches near Messines. The orders puzzled Edward: Trenches were a poor target for bombing from the altitude where the planes would be safe from rifle and machine-gun fire. Why risk valuable aircraft for the faint hope of blasting some poor beggars buried in the mud of trenches? But orders were orders, and Edward soon forgot about the puzzle in his concern for Wooley. Last night he had heard furniture breaking in Doggo's room, and the big redhead had not appeared for breakfast. In Fortescue's present state he was capable of court-martialing a man who failed to fly an assigned mission.

Edward was about to take over the mission when Doggo came around the hangar, pulling on his gloves, and strode without a word to his plane. Edward walked over and watched as his friend climbed into the cockpit and fastened his safety belt. Wooley's face was grim but he seemed in control of himself.

"I'm going to fly your tail," Edward said off-handedly. "To hell with the major." Wooley did not turn his head, only nodded to show that he had heard.

The patrol was routine right up to the last bombing pass over the trenches. As Edward had suspected, the bombs fell far from their target, adding a few more craters to the pockmarked terrain. It was a ridiculous waste.

Suddenly Doggo rocked his wings violently and

jabbed a gloved hand up and to the rear. Intent on watching the bombs fall, Edward had failed to search the sky behind him. Now he turned and saw the enemy planes curving down not two hundred yards away. Cursing himself for not being alert, he armed his guns and prepared to follow Doggo's maneuvers.

The British formation dissolved as the gaily painted Fokkers dove through, guns blazing. By a miracle, no one went down under the first attack. As Wooley climbed sharply, Edward followed, hanging grimly onto his flight leader's tail. This was a *Jagdstaffel* new to the sector—painted in circus colors but all with red tails. *Well, let's see how good they are.*

Wooley dove on two Fokkers that had a Bristol Scout hemmed in. Edward followed him down, hanging back and watching alertly for any interference. Two more Fokkers broke away from the melee below and climbed to intercept the flight leader. Before they had gained enough altitude to be a real threat, Edward turned and cut in front of them, his machine guns blazing. The two German pilots banked away, trying to get around the annoying British plane, but Edward was everywhere, twisting and turning to keep them off Doggo's tail. Finally the Fokkers gave up and went off in search of easier prey.

When Edward turned back to find Wooley, the flight commander was sticking to the tail of the second Fokker. His first victim was already spiraling down, trailing a long black smoke plume. Edward took up his position again, scanning the

skies in all directions. The other three Bristols
were holding their own, for half the enemy formation had gone to attack the pesky bombers. Hold
on to Doggo's tail, Edward told himself. Let's see
if this tactic works.

Once more he chased an enemy plane off, firing
short bursts across its nose until it turned away.
By that time, Wooley had claimed his second kill,
and the two Scouts had flung themselves down to
help the others. But the Germans had had enough.
They had lost three planes and had gotten only
one of the bombers—the other two were safely
out of reach—so as the two British planes dropped
down the German leader rocked his wings and
led his men in a steep dive for home. The Bristols
re-formed triumphantly and sped south.

It works, Edward exulted. Damn Fortescue anyway. He wondered if any of the other pilots in
Red Flight had seen the new tactic in action.
Probably not. They had been too busy with their
own dogfights.

After they landed, he and Doggo agreed to say
nothing about two-plane teams for fear that the
major would prohibit them, but they also agreed
that all of Red Flight would now use this way of
air combat.

The war went on and on. In March the Tsar of
All the Russias abdicated. In April the United
States entered the war, but there was little time
to rejoice over the new ally. April 1917 was to be
known among the pilots of the Royal Flying Corps
as "Bloody April." In thirty merciless days almost

half of the fliers of the RFC were killed, wounded, or missing in action.

The month began badly. The British Army was preparing a large offensive at Arras and demanded that the air be cleared of German observation planes that might spot the buildup. For five days prior to the advance the RFC fought desperately against overwhelming odds to carry out that mission. Outclassed in equipment, almost helpless against superior Albatros and Fokker fighters, the British squadrons suffered defeat after defeat. Although Arras was south of their assigned sector, Number Twenty-four Squadron was called in to help in the hopeless struggle. And the losses were in vain, for when the British troops left their trenches and moved unflinchingly across no-man's-land, they found the German positions empty. The enemy had retreated to a stronger fortified line far to the rear.

Every day that the weather allowed, Red Flight flew aggressive patrols, searching for and attacking any German observation planes in the air. No sooner would they spot their target and dive to intercept when the skies would be filled with enemy fighters, always in superior numbers. For the first time they were faced with the famous Von Richthofen squadron, top aces all, rising from their base at Douai to claim their victims. The Red Baron himself was present in several of these encounters, and twice Edward drove the well-known all-red Fokker triplane off Doggo's tail.

In the brutal slaughter of April only Red Flight seemed to be exempt. While the rest of the RFC was losing an average of ten pilots and observers a day, Wooley's flight lost one, a new man who bravely left his rear position to attack three triplanes. The flight shot down seven German planes. Doggo himself shot down four, making him the squadron's top ace, with nine victories. The other pilots in the squadron began to remark about "lucky Red Flight," and although Fortescue may have had his suspicions about this success, he said nothing. After all, Wing headquarters had praised his command lavishly.

But Number Twenty-four did not escape unscathed. The empty chairs in the mess at night mocked the commendations from headquarters. The adjutant who received reports on the losses in all RFC squadrons gave up trying to estimate the average life expectancy of a pilot on the Western Front. It was too horrifying to contemplate. The new pilots who arrived were almost useless in the air. Most of them had less than ten hours solo, and more than half had never even flown a Bristol Scout. Like the other veterans, Edward tried to tell them how to survive in a dogfight, but they never lasted long enough to learn.

In the beginning of May the battle sputtered to a halt as the exhausted troops dug in again. New Sopwith Camels arrived, and Edward was busy teaching the other pilots the tricks of flying a rotary-engine plane. After his daily patrol he would get the men into the air for simulated combat, teaching the two-plane tactic when the major was absent. It was accepted enthusiastically by the other pilots as the secret of Red Flight's success.

Edward's diary for June 5, 1917:

> In four weeks, the squadron has changed drastically. Everyone loves the new planes and with the new tactics the odds are beginning to shift in our favor. We were shot out of the air in April, but now we are holding our own—and a bit more. Doggo got his eleventh victory today and is up for the Military Cross. I got my ninth confirmed kill, an Albatros who tried to sneak under me to get at Doggo. My guns broke his main spar and the wing collapsed and down he went like a broken bird. Strange, I had no feeling about it at all—almost as if it were someone else who pressed the trigger. This war has gone on too long. It's becoming a habit.
>
> A storm is moving in from the Channel and will cover this sector for two days. Doggo and I are going on leave to Amiens. Good food, soft beds, and no dawn patrols. Lovely thought.

"Edouard?" The soft feminine voice was insistent, cajoling.

Edward stared up at the dark ceiling, trying to recall the ornate plaster design. The Hôtel du Rhin in Amiens had been very fashionable before the war, but now it was touched by the shabbiness of neglect. Still, the kitchen was marvelous and the staff was genuinely fond of the British fliers and tolerant of their boisterous ways. Fortescue had insisted they stay at this hotel, which had one of the few telephones in the town. He wanted to be certain that he could recall his pilots if need be.

"Tu dors, chéri?" No, Yvette, thought Edward, I'm not asleep—just thinking. About you, about Ann. There is a great deal to ponder, and besides I'm not very sleepy. You're very sweet, and I wish my French were good enough so I could tell you all that you've meant to me. But it does raise a problem, you see. I haven't had much experience with women, what with the war and all, and I thought that Ann was the only one for me. So what am I doing in the Hôtel du Rhin with a lovely French girl breathing in my ear at three o'clock in the morning?

He kissed her gently, then slid out from under the covers and went to the window. The room was hot and stuffy, so he drew back the heavy curtains and opened the window. The air was cool, and he breathed deeply and gratefully. Behind him he heard a rustle of sheets as Yvette snuggled deeper into the bed. He stared out at the dark roofs of the town and thought gratefully of the sleeping girl. He owed her a great deal; for two days she had helped him forget the war.

Yesterday afternoon, shortly after their arrival in Amiens, Doggo had left him sitting in a restaurant and had disappeared for thirty minutes. When he returned he had two French girls on his arms, and their beauty had taken Edward's breath away. Armande was petite, dark, with flashing eyes and a clever line of chatter. Yvette was taller, fairer, with wheat-colored hair and hazel eyes— more serious, quieter. Luckily Doggo spoke a fair French, so the luncheon had gone famously. The girls worked for the French War Ministry in Amiens as typists in a truck factory.

Edward was embarrassed by his own awkward silence as Doggo and Armande chatted away happily. He smiled tentatively at Yvette and offered her some wine. She nodded gravely and continued to stare at him in the most disconcerting fashion. What an idiot she must think me, Edward thought miserably. Why can't I say something gallant or amusing? Why didn't I pay more attention to my French in school?

It was Saturday, and the girls were free in the afternoon. They had walked through the park, had dined in a small bistro that Armande swore had the best food in Amiens, then had taken the girls to a British Army cinema, where Doggo gallantly tried to translate the captions of an old Douglas Fairbanks thriller. Yvette stared poker-faced at the screen without a word. Edward felt more gauche and uncomfortable all the time.

The next morning they had picked the girls up at their pension and had walked along the Somme River. It was drizzling and windy, but the two young couples did not mind. Edward was making progress with a mixture of gestures and broken French, and once or twice he got a slight smile from the lovely Yvette.

After lunch the two girls had taken them to the cathedral—"worried about our souls," Doggo grumbled—and had knelt with them in the semi-darkness of the vaulting nave. Edward remembered something from his history lessons: Edward the Third had gone to mass here on his way to Crécy. Not a bad idea for another Briton to pray here before going back to the war. Doggo continued to mutter about a waste of time, but Armande gave him a sharp elbow in the ribs and he dutifully bent his head.

There was a strange odor in the church, something more pungent than dust and the smoke from the candles. On the way out, Edward identified it. Part of the cathedral had been converted into a field hospital. The wounded were on stretchers in the chapels and sacristy, surrounded by the biting odor of antiseptic. The girls crossed themselves, but the two pilots only stared stonily. They did not want to be reminded of the war—not yet.

At dinner, Yvette said something quietly to Edward, but he shook his head. "I'm sorry, mademoiselle. I don't understand."

Doggo grinned. "She asked if you have a girl, a fiancée, someone you love."

Edward fiddled with his wineglass, afraid to meet Yvette's eyes. He thought of Ann and her long silence, the bitter thought that she might have met someone else and had forgotten him. All the anger of the last months waiting for a letter from her that never came welled up in him. If he was not going to survive this war—and the odds were that he would not—well, he wasn't going to miss this chance moping over a girl who had forgotten him. He was not so naïve as to miss the promise in Yvette's question.

"Tell her no," he said to Wooley. "No girl, no fiancée, no one."

"*Pas d'amie, pas de fiancée—personne,*" Doggo translated. "And this is our last night . . . eh, *ce soir est notre dernier soir . . . demain, nous rentrons* . . . we go back to the war, understand?"

Yvette nodded gravely and took Edward's hand. Armande began to weep until Yvette spoke to her sharply.

Late that night, in the darkness of his room, he and Yvette made love. For Edward, it was the first time. When it was over, she slept and he stared at the ceiling, half grateful and half guilty. Try as he may, there was still the thought of Ann. He had lied to Yvette. There was another girl.

Standing at the window, he stared out over the sodden rooftops of Amiens. Not a light showed, for fear of air raids, but a dim moonlight filtered through the thin clouds. It's breaking up, he thought. Tomorrow we'll be flying again. Well, at least that hadn't been a lie. Tomorrow he and Doggo would go back to the squadron.

Suddenly a line of bright blue light flashed in the north, throwing the houses into sharp relief. It trembled and died, but another sprang up, then another. Amazed, Edward searched the skies for some explanation. Bombs? An ammunition dump going up? Then the booming sound of the explosions reached them as three blast waves sped over the town. Windows were thrown open and anxious white faces peered out. Wrapped in a sheet, Yvette appeared beside him and asked the obvious question.

"Don't know," Edward said. "*Sais pas*. Never saw anything like that before."

There was a timid knock on the door. As Edward opened it the hall porter bowed apologetically and said, "*Le téléphone, mon lieutenant*." Edward nodded and closed the door. He dressed hastily and went down to the reception desk.

It was the adjutant. "Sorry to cut your leave short, Burton, but you and Wooley are to return at once. I'm sure you heard the bang just now. Well, we've exploded some mines under the German trenches at Messines and our troops are advancing at this moment. It was all very hush-hush and we've just got the word. Every plane is to be in the air at dawn. There'll be a truck in front of the hotel in twenty minutes. Get the word to Doggo like a good chap. Good-bye."

On the way back to the room he passed a sleepy Wooley standing in the hall in his pajamas, scratching his head. Behind him a frightened Armande, beautiful in a thin robe, peered out over his shoulder. "What's happening, old boy?" Doggo yawned.

Edward explained the orders quickly. "Better get dressed, Doggo. We leave in less than twenty minutes. Besides, the French take a dim view of scantily clad couples roaming around public corridors. The major will have your hide if some bluenose complains."

"Perfect defense," Doggo grinned. "Obeying

King's Regulations. Paragraph 36, section 2: 'Athletic contests. An officer shall be at all times properly dressed for the sport in which he is engaged.' "

The truck was on time, and while the porter and driver were loading their kit Edward and Doggo said separate and private farewells. Yvette listened carefully to Edward's words without understanding a single one, then she kissed him softly twice. He took off his silver identification bracelet and put it into her hand. "Yvette, this is . . . to remember me by . . . Doggo! How do you say 'to remember me by'?"

"*Pour le souvenir*," Doggo's muffled voice said out of the darkness on the other side of the truck.

"*Pour le souvenir*," Edward repeated. Yvette nodded gravely and kissed him again.

From the rear of the truck he caught a last glimpse of her standing on the hotel steps waving. Armande was beside her, waving and clutching a handkerchief to her lips.

Then the truck turned the corner and they were gone.

6

The main road behind Courtrai was jammed with German troops, trucks, and wagons moving up to contain the English breakthrough. Under the hot sun, surrounded by a cloud of brown dust kicked up by thousands of feet and tires, they looked to Edward like an army of gray-green ants. What a target, he thought.

He threw a hasty glance over his right shoulder to check on the others. Bouncing in the turbulent air behind him, two khaki Camels clung to his tail. Red Flights Three and Five, Lieutenants Morris and Jeffreys on the squadron roster, followed Edward—Red Flight Two—across the rooftops of Courtrai, skimming the chimneys to stay hidden as long as possible. Off to the left, Doggo and Red Flight Four were curving low over the Lys canal to attack the head of the enemy column. It had been Wooley's idea to split the flight and confuse the Germans by hitting them at two different points.

Edward led his two planes down across an open field, signaling them to spread out for the attack. As they pulled up over a line of tall poplars the road was directly in front of them. The nearest German troops froze as the three Camels roared up over the trees and plunged down toward them. *Why don't they run?*

The hammering of the six British machine guns deafened Edward, and the nearest section of the road disappeared in a fountain of dirty brown jets. Little red flashes in their midst showed where the copper-jacketed bullets had hit metal. Scores of small gray-green figures did a grim dance amid the smoke puffs, twisting, falling, clutching their bodies or reaching futilely into the air as if to stop the bullets with their bare hands. A truck exploded, throwing out streamers of orange flame. Out of the corner of his eye, Edward saw soldiers running toward a machine gun mounted on the flat bed of a truck. Horses bolted, dragging their wagons off the road and into the safety of the fields.

Then the Camels were past the road and climbing clear. As they turned to continue the attack, Edward saw Doggo and Red Flight Four hitting the head of the column just as it was entering the town. He looked around anxiously for Jerry fighters. At this altitude the Camels would have no chance at all; but the skies were empty.

By the time the British planes returned to the road the troops had abandoned the trucks and wagons and were hidden in the ditches. They sent up intensive rifle and machine-gun fire, and Edward cringed as tracers whipped about his plane. He banked sharply to throw off the gunners' aim and lined up with the road. Firing steadily, he flew down the column of deserted trucks, setting fire to some and blowing others apart. Those he missed were left to his two wingmen. At the end of the column, their ammunition gone, the three Camels curved up to two thousand feet and set a course for home. They would rendezvous with the rest of Red Flight south of Courtrai, but now speed was essential. Their machine-gun belts were empty, and if attacked they could only run and pray.

Wooley and his partner joined them five minutes later. The planes fell naturally into a vee formation with Doggo at the point and Edward off his right wing. There was nothing ragged about their flying. They were veterans, survivors in the deadliest game in the world. They flew as if their lives depended upon it—because they did. Turning their heads constantly, they scanned every sector of the sky for the first sign of the enemy. Here a split-second advance warning of a hostile plane was the difference between living or dying.

The Camels crossed the lines just east of Messines. Edward looked down and saw the gaping white craters left by the mine explosions in the soft chalk ground of Flanders. British troops were clinging to the rim, waiting for the enemy assault. Beneath the uneven floor of the three gigantic holes untold numbers of German soldiers were entombed. Edward could not help wondering what that last moment had been like as the earth beneath their feet had heaved upward, tearing some to bits and burying others forever. One million pounds of high explosives. The British sappers had worked like moles for eight months silently preparing this trap.

As they landed at Saint-Omer, Blue Flight was warming up on the tarmac, getting set to continue the strafing of German reinforcements. The struts of the lead plane carried the squadron commander's red streamers—Fortescue was taking advantage of his right to join any flight at any time. As Edward taxied up to the hangar line he saw Foley standing by the major's cockpit shouting something in his ear. Under his goggles, Fortescue's face was stiff and unyielding. His answer must have been curt, for the sergeant-major stiffened, saluted, turned on his heel, and strode away angrily. More trouble, Edward thought. It's got to be very bad if he antagonizes even Foley.

After filling out his report in the operations office—"Enemy regiment, trucks, and wagons successfully attacked on the Courtrai road. Heavy damage inflicted"—Edward went to find Foley. The sergeant-major was talking to a mechanic in the repair shed when Edward walked up. The mechanic discreetly disappeared, leaving the two men alone.

"Trouble, Sergeant-Major?" Edward asked softly. Foley set his jaw and stared at his clipboard before answering. "Begging the lieutenant's pardon, I'd rather not discuss the major's affairs with anyone but the major."

Edward paused to wipe some oil from his cheek. "Fair enough. But the major's 'affairs' concern the rest of this squadron vitally. We have to help the C.O. as best we can, but we have to know how. What's the problem?"

Foley shifted uncomfortably, reluctant to carry tales. He would never have talked about it to a new pilot, but Burton was an old hand. He had flown with Number Four back when they had more to fear from their own flimsy machines than from the enemy.

"It's Sergeant Daley, sir, the armorer. The major has him up on charges for neglect of duty. Seems the major's machine guns were being stripped and cleaned this morning when he came out to fly. Daley swears that he was not told that the major was going out with Blue Flight today, but the C.O. cursed him in front of the men, called him a liar, and has signed court-martial charges. A bad business, sir; the men are very upset. You know Daley, Lieutenant—a good man, very conscientious. Very popular with the others. He'd never strip the major's guns before a flight."

"Where's Daley now?"

"The major made him reassemble the guns, then sent him to his quarters under arrest. Damned miserable he is too. He was due for leave next week. Hasn't seen his wife and son for over seven months."

Edward nodded thoughtfully. "All right, Sergeant-Major. Leave this to me."

"Begging the lieutenant's pardon, but do you think you should concern yourself with this? The major's not very fond of you as it is. He'll not take kindly to your interfering with discipline."

"This isn't discipline, this is a commanding officer going off his rocker and destroying squadron morale." Edward was angry, not at Foley and not even at Fortescue, but at the rotten system that kept a man under the torture of command until he gave way. "Don't worry. I'll try to be tactful. I'm not anxious for a court-martial myself."

In the lounge, Edward found Doggo leering at the pictures in a bawdy French magazine, a cigar and a stiff drink of brandy beside him. Taking the magazine out of his hands and cutting off his protests, Edward quickly explained Sergeant Daley's situation.

Wooley scratched his head and groaned. "Can't see what we can do about this, Edward. The C.O. is king in his own squadron. He can line us all up and shoot us, and Wing would only send him more men."

"But Fortescue is breaking up, Doggo. He's destroying morale not only among the officers but among the enlisted men as well. Any day now he'll go off the deep end and we'll be in the soup for real."

"So what do we do, being loyal officers of the King and all that?"

Edward's voice was low and determined. He glanced around the room to make certain that no one could hear. "I could go to headquarters and request that a medical board examine Fortescue."

Wooley practically leaped out of his chair. He stared open-mouthed at his friend.

"My God, Edward, are you mad? Do you know what Wing would make of that—an officer asking them to find out if his C.O. is balmy? Mutiny, that's what—insubordination, action prejudicial to military discipline, at the very least. Do you really think they will admit that they've left a sick man in command of a squadron at the front for over a year, giving life or death orders? They'd never do that—think of what the newspapers would make of it if they found out. No, Wing would crucify us and bury us somewhere quietly. They've got to protect Fortescue."

Edward smiled warmly. Without realizing it, Doggo had said "us," not "you." The big, bluff Yorkshireman had already bought himself a piece of the coming trouble, but he would have been offended if Edward had thanked him.

"I'm not going to Wing," Edward said. "This is a matter for the commanding general. I'm going to RFC headquarters at Saint André to see General Trenchard."

Doggo slumped in his chair and raised his eyes to the ceiling in a mute appeal for help against such insanity. He took a deep swallow of his brandy before answering. "I'll have a car standing by after dinner. We can't leave before then. I don't suppose that we need ask the major's permission, since we are only going to try to get him certified as a loony?"

Shaking his head, Edward reached for the cigar and placed it between Doggo's lips. Then he left to prepare a letter that would undoubtedly make General Trenchard furious.

*   *   *

He was still sweating over the letter when he heard Blue Flight returning. For a moment he thought of going out and telling Fortescue his plan. He hated the idea of sneaking behind the major's back. The man had been his teacher, his model, his first flying instructor—this was a strange way to pay him back. But Edward knew it would be a useless gesture. The major would simply put him under arrest and see that he never left the field except to fly. My first duty is to the squadron, Edward thought. For the good of the squadron, Fortescue must give up the command.

He slid the letter into the table drawer and went out to watch the flight come in. They were circling over the south end of the field, beginning their approach. Edward counted them: four—one man gone. One by one the Camels dropped down with a blipping sound, rolled across the field, slowed, turned, and taxied to the tarmac. With a shock Edward realized that none of the four planes bore the red streamers. His head was buzzing and there was a tight feeling in his chest. It was Fortescue— the major had not come back.

He ran up to meet the incoming planes. Leading Blue Flight Two was Andrews, the ex-lawyer from Cardiff, at thirty the oldest pilot in the squadron. When his plane stopped, Edward was at the cockpit shouting, "The major! What happened?" Behind him pilots and mechanics crowded around, shouting the same question.

Andrews raised his goggles and wiped his oil-flecked face with his gloved hand. Reaching down, he flipped off the ignition switch. The engine sputtered and died. The propeller slowed and stopped.

"He's dead," Andrews said tersely. "On a strafing run." He got down from the cockpit and pushed his way through the buzzing crowd without another word. Edward followed him into the operations shack, knowing better than to ask more questions of an exhausted man.

It all came out as Andrews gave his report to the adjutant in the crowded, smoky room. Blue Flight had found another German infantry column moving toward Roulers. On the major's signal they had attacked in single file, sweeping low across the road and firing in turn. The first attack had been devastating, and then they had climbed and turned for a second sweep. What had happened then still puzzled Andrews.

"The C.O. came down along the road, firing in short bursts. I could see his bullets raking the ditches where the Jerries were huddled. There was a long black lorry ahead of him with twin machine guns. He headed for it and it disappeared in the dust kicked up by his guns. It exploded—but the major never stopped firing. He kept diving toward it and riddling it with bullets when the only thing you could see was a big flaming cloud."

Andrews paused and swallowed hard. "He never came out of the dive. His plane went right into the burning lorry and blew up."

There was a stunned silence in the room, then someone cursed under his breath. Edward felt sick. *Poor Allen, what a terrible end. If I had acted sooner, he might have been saved.*

The adjutant picked up the telephone to pass the report on to Wing. There was a long wait while they searched for the brigadier.

Andrews drew a map from the leg pocket of his flying suit and circled the fatal spot in red. "That's where he went down. He must have been hit by the machine-gun fire as he attacked. No other explanation for it." The adjutant nodded. So that will be the official report, Edward thought. Nothing will be said about a man pushed beyond his strength. That business with Daley must have been the final straw. Confused, despairing, desperate . . . and all he had to do was not pull back on the stick and it was all over.

The adjutant spoke briefly to the brigadier, telling him of Fortescue's death, then he turned and handed Wooley the telephone. "He wants to talk to the senior flight commander, Doggo. Orders for tomorrow."

Wooley spat out his cigar and picked up the telephone as if it were a poisonous snake. "Captain Wooley here, sir. Yes, sir, I understand . . . the Courtrai sector again. Yes, sir. Thank you, sir. We'll do our best."

And so it goes on. No time to mourn Allen Fortescue or pity Doggo. Business as usual. Edward walked out of the room and stood watching the mechanics swarm over the Blue Flight planes, patching holes, refueling, running long, snaking ammunition belts up to the guns. Doggo came out alone a few minutes later and stood beside him. They did not speak for several minutes.

Finally Doggo cleared his throat and said, "Red Flight goes out at dawn to strafe in the Courtrai sector. You lead. I'm assigning Billy Carpenter to your flight. Good luck. Oh yes, I've torn up the charges against Daley. Sent him back to duty."

Edward watched Wooley stride toward the headquarters building. *And good luck to you, Doggo, my friend. We'll both need it.* He wondered if Wooley would do any better as C.O. than Fortescue had. And how well would he, Edward, command Red Flight?

Summer faded and autumn arrived with chill mornings and gusty winds. The leaves turned and now the landscape was a mosaic of yellows and reds, and the fields were filled with ripening wheat. The soldiers ignored the colorful changes and fought on.

Doggo Wooley was promoted to major, and his command of the squadron was confirmed. He ordered every flight to practice and use the two-plane tactic, and slowly the tide of battle in the air shifted. The new planes—the Camels and the S.E. 5s—could hold their own against the latest Albatroses and Fokkers, and although the new pilots were not much better than before, Wooley had time to teach them some tricks before sending them over the lines. With experienced wingmen they managed to last through the first dogfights, and that made them veterans fast.

Red Flight was still the lucky flight in the Twenty-fourth. As soon as he assumed command, Edward set stern rules for air discipline: No tail man was to leave his position, no matter how tempting a target was sighted; no victory rolls over the airfield—a Blue Flight plane had lost a wing doing that; constant alertness at all times, even on the return flight; and last but not least, no drinking six hours or less before flying. When the veterans, Morris and Jeffreys, objected, Edward coldly invited them to request a transfer to another flight. When the two stubborn pilots went in to Wooley with their request, he damned them to hell and sent them back chastened to Red Flight.

Billy Carpenter was the one weak spot. He was a good flier, but inexperienced, and he lacked the ability for instant decision necessary for survival. Every day after their patrol, Edward had Carpenter in the air with him, practicing acrobatics in simulated combat. To improve the new man's marksmanship, Edward would dump out a dozen empty cans and make Carpenter follow them down firing to see how many he could hit before they struck the ground. Until he was satisfied, Edward protected Billy Carpenter's tail on their patrols over the lines.

There was a lull in the trench fighting in October and November as the two armies licked their wounds and planned the next offensive. The French were willing to wait for the masses of fresh troops, guns, and planes from the United States, but the British High Command was still hoping for the great breakthrough that would end the war before Christmas. "It was supposed to be the Christmas of 1914," Andrews observed sourly. The Germans, seeing victory slip from their grasp, were desperate. The next offensive would have to be decisive, for they were scraping the bottom of their manpower pool. Their best general, Ludendorff, spent hours hunched over his maps, searching for the weak point in the Allied lines.

In the air the German squadrons only attacked when the odds were overwhelmingly in their favor. Otherwise they were under orders to stay out of dogfights and keep up their strength in planes and veteran pilots. As the autumn advanced, fewer and fewer German fighters came up to challenge the RFC. Soon winter set in with its storms, sleet, and high winds, and flying ceased for days on end. But the quiet was deceptive. In the trenches the "normal wastage" in dead and wounded still went on.

Late one evening Edward was sitting in his room reading a letter from Yvette. It had been handed to him by a new pilot who had passed through Amiens on his way to the squadron. "This smashing girl came up to me and handed me this letter, pointing to the name on the envelope: Lieutenant E. Burton, 24 Squadron, Saint-Omer. I assured her as best I could that it would be delivered. What a lovely girl! You're a lucky bloke, Burton." Edward winced as he remembered a lanky Scots sergeant who had said those same words when he saw Ann waiting on the dock at Dover. He took the letter and went to his room.

It was written in a clear, slanted hand on light blue paper that was slightly scented. With the help of a dictionary Edward was able to get the sense of it without too much difficulty. *"Mon cher Edouard"* it began. First came regrets about not having written sooner, but *la poste militaire*— that would be the army post office—would not accept letters from civilians. "I often think of you and pray for your safety." Edward saw her kneeling in the cathedral, her head bent. "Now I must tell you something that may . . ." *te froisser,* what the hell is that? *Oh yes,* "hurt you." "My fiancé has returned from a German prisoner-of-war camp after two years of captivity. He has lost a leg and the Boches know that he cannot fight again. We are being married in two weeks." *My God, her fiancé!* "Do not think"—*think what?*—"too harshly of me, for I was very lonely and for a time I did love you, even though I knew there was always another in your heart. Good-bye. *Mille baisers"*— *a thousand kisses?*

Edward sniffed the scented paper and thought about the dark hotel room in Amiens. So she knew that he had lied and still she had loved him. He put the letter carefully in his diary. He knew that he would never forget Yvette. He never wanted to forget her.

The next day Wooley called Edward into his office and handed him his promotion orders. "Congratulations, *Captain* Burton," Doggo said with a smile. In the old days a third pip would have called for a round of drinks and a drunken brawl in the mess hall, but the squadron had changed.

It was more sober, more professional, more businesslike. Promotions were like losses—inevitable with the passage of time. "Like medals," the old Doggo had once said. "The only way to avoid getting them is to either get yourself killed or commit suicide." Wooley shook his hand and dismissed him.

Outside the office the adjutant added his congratulations. Catching Edward's thoughtful look back at the C.O.'s door, the adjutant said quietly, "A commanding officer doesn't have friends, Burton. It's hard enough sending up men who are only names to you, but a friend . . . ?" Was I Fortescue's friend? Edward wondered. Did I help to break him?

"By the way, Burton," the adjutant said, "are you acquainted with a General Masterman?" Startled, Edward could only nod.

"He's at RFC headquarters now, in charge of personnel," the adjutant continued. "He did his damnedest to kill your promotion, but General Trenchard saw the list and demanded to know why your name was not on it. Masterman had to write it in himself under the commanding general's watchful eye."

"Masterman thinks I talk too much to reporters," Edward said.

The adjutant laughed. "Oh, that old business. Well, 'Boom' Trenchard told him in his iciest tone that the next time a deserving young officer was denied promotion because of a personal grudge, the officer responsible would be counting spare parts in a warehouse in Le Havre for the rest of the war. That wilted Masterman more than a bit."

Sergeant-Major Foley marched in in his best parade manner, came to a jolting halt before Edward, and saluted proudly. Edward returned the salute and smiled. "Well, Sergeant-Major," he asked, "did you ever think that the raw recruit you taught to stand up straight and walk in a military manner would ever be a captain in the Royal Flying Corps?"

"Begging the captain's pardon," Foley said gruffly, "there were times when I was most discouraged about the prospects—but I always had me hopes."

"Thank you, Sergeant-Major, for everything."

Edward's diary for December 21, 1917:

> Bad weather for the last two days and it is going to continue. Most of the pilots have gone to Amiens on forty-eight-hour passes, but I refused mine. I was afraid that I might meet Yvette and her fiancé. That would be painful for all three of us—if she's told him. I had a letter from Mr. Ogilvie today. Ann has been very ill, Spanish influenza. She's recovering now but has just received another bad blow. Her cousin, Peter McIlvain, a young naval sublieutenant, was lost when his destroyer was torpedoed and sunk off the Faroes last week. Ann is taking this very hard. She had grown up with Peter and was very fond of him. With Iain and Peter gone—

and with her concern for me—she is very
depressed.

("I worry about her state of mind, Edward," her
father had written. "She sits for hours doing nothing but staring into the fireplace. Please write to
her. You must know that you still mean a great
deal to her. Our prayers are for your safety and
quick return. Affectionately, Thomas Ogilvie.")

Edward wrote the same day a long, loving plea
for forgiveness and to let Ann know that he had
never stopped thinking of her—which was true—
and that he had been faithful—which was not.
There had been a twinge of guilt as he wrote this,
but he believed that his feeling for Yvette had
nothing to do with his love for Ann. The encounter
in Amiens had taken place because he had thought
that Ann was lost to him.

The day after Christmas the skies cleared and
Edward led Red Flight on an offensive sweep over
the lines. Enemy fighters were still strangely absent, and the only hostile plane they spotted was
a Rumpler two-seater taking photographs near
Ypres. It fled as soon as they started to dive, and
it was under the protection of the German anti-
aircraft guns before the Camels were in range.
Edward signaled the flight to re-form. They
cruised back and forth five thousand feet above
the trenches, but no Albatroses or Fokkers came
up to fight. Edward looked over at his wingman,
Billy Carpenter, now holding his position like a
veteran, and held up his hands in puzzlement.
Carpenter grinned broadly and pointed down at

the Rumpler, but Edward shook his head. Too risky with all those guns around. There was nothing in this sector that had to be protected from the Jerries. Let them take all the photographs they wanted. But where were their damned fighters?

After another hour of aimless flying up and down the line Edward signaled the return to base. All the way to Saint-Omer he worried about the apparent reluctance of the *Jagdstaffels* to dispute the mastery of the skies. The Jerries were saving their planes for a big push—no doubt about it— but where and when?

Doggo was in the operations room when Edward came in to fill out his report. Edward mentioned the lone observation plane and the continued absence of any fighter opposition. "We'll have to attack their airfields if we want to keep them from hiding," Edward said. "That might put a crimp in their plans."

Wooley grunted as he lit a cigar. "You can be certain that they'll be ready for that. Rather an obvious idea. Heavy losses for us. Besides, they've probably dispersed their planes far to the rear. They'll bring them back just before the attack."

Edward agreed. He signed his report, then went to his quarters. There was no mail for him, but it was too early to expect an answer from Ann. Mr. Ogilvie's letter had taken eight days to arrive.

Edward's diary for January 1, 1918:

New Year's Day. Cold and clear. Wind 12 miles per hour out of the west. Everyone is getting jumpy about the disappearance of the enemy planes. We know that a big attack is coming. The Germans can't wait much longer or the Americans will be here in force and then they will have lost the war. It's the waiting that's hardest to take. Why don't they begin? Still no letter from Ann.

"Edward?" The voice was gruff and slurred. Edward opened his eyes and stared into the darkness. There was a smell of brandy.

"Hello, Doggo. What time is it?"

"About three, old man. Sorry. I know you have the dawn patrol, but I couldn't sleep." Edward grunted and sat up, rubbing his eyes.

Wooley fumbled around and forced a glass of brandy in Edward's hand. "Happy birthday, Edward. Safe landings and all that. You're one of the best."

Edward grinned to himself in the dark and sipped the drink. He had forgotten today was his twentieth birthday. But Doggo had remembered. Good old Doggo.

They sat in silence for a while. There was a gurgling sound as Wooley refilled his glass.

"I'm sorry about the way it is, old man," Doggo said morosely. "Damn lonely job being a C.O. No friends, no one to talk to—just give orders to a lot of fine chaps and send them up to get killed. Lousy job. Know now why Fortescue went off the deep end. Sitting around while other men are up fighting."

"Come off it, Doggo," Edward protested. "You

do as much flying as any man in this squadron—
and run the outfit too. Nothing for you to feel
guilty about. Someone has to do it."

"Nice of you to say so, old man. Miss you, but
can't have favorites, you know. Bad for the others.
Bad for morale. No friends—just give orders and
up they go. Miss you, though. Lots of fun together,
you and I. Amiens, remember Amiens?"

"Yes." *I will always remember Amiens, but not
for the town.*

They talked for fifteen minutes, remembering
good times and bad: Edward's first victory, an
Aviatik in October 1914; the day Doggo was shot
down and arrived back at the squadron covered
with hay; the men they had known who had
been killed or wounded—a long list, that one.
Doggo drank steadily, but Edward refused to allow
his glass to be refilled—"I have to fly in two
hours, Doggo, and you know I don't have your
head for this stuff."

Finally Wooley stood up and said softly, "Get
some sleep, old man. I need you. You're doing a
great job with Red Flight. I need you, old boy.
Don't get yourself killed."

Aghast, Edward watched the bulky form move
toward the door. *God, he must be drunk. It's
strictly taboo to say that to a man before a combat
mission. The worst kind of luck.* But Edward knew
that Doggo drank to keep from cracking up under
the strain of command.

"G'night, Edward." The door closed before Edward could reply. He got out of bed and emptied
the remains of his drink into the washbasin. His

heart was pounding and all idea of sleep was gone. He was not superstitious, like some of the pilots with their lucky beads and scarves and silk stockings. But this . . .

As Edward stood beside his plane, watching the first orange streaks of dawn on the horizon, the adjutant came up with final orders. Usually Doggo gave the last-minute instructions, but the C.O. was unavailable, the adjutant said with a nervous laugh. Then he leaned forward and whispered into Edward's ear. "Word came in late last night that Doggo's brother is dead. Trench mortar. Killed instantly."

Edward nodded and climbed into the cockpit. As he fastened his safety belt he noticed that his hands were trembling. *Poor Doggo. Poor all of us.*

"Switch off?" The mechanic's call roused him.

"Switch off," he answered. The propeller was swung through twice. "Switch on?" *Yes, damn you, the switch is on.*

The engine caught on the first pull-through. Edward let it warm for a minute, then raised his glove hand above his head and pointed forward.

One by one the planes of Red Flight taxied out from the tarmac and followed their leader to the takeoff strip.

The war went on.

7

Edward's diary for January 16, 1918:

> Ann's letter arrived today! She asks me to forgive her and to try to understand how hurt she was by my decision to return to the war. During her illness she had had a lot of time to think. When her cousin was killed, she realized that the war left no time for recriminations, that it was important to grasp at happiness, at whatever hours might be granted us. The only thing that matters is that she loves me! God, for the first time in over a year, I'm happy!

Billy Carpenter died quickly, which Edward later thought was a mercy since his plane burned like a Roman candle all the way down until it buried itself into a hill behind Messines. One second he was hurrying to catch up with Red Flight after falling far behind. The next second his body was jerking against the safety belt; he was dead before his head hit the instrument panel. He never saw the three red-tailed Fokkers behind him.

Edward had been watching the bombers on their last run over the woods. Intelligence had located a German ammunition dump there: mounds of shells, cannon, and trucks, all carefully hidden under camouflage nets. Now the clumsy five-hundred-pound bombs had begun to rain down on the woods.

The chatter of the Spandau machine guns as they riddled Carpenter's cockpit caused an automatic reflex action in Edward. Even as he threw a glance over his shoulder to identify the threat, he pulled back on the control stick and hit hard right rudder, sending the Camel into a screaming tight chandelle. In a flash he knew that the flight was in deep trouble: Three Fokkers were diving on him through the oily black plume that marked Carpenter's last dive, seven more were closing quickly on his left. Ten against five—hopeless odds.

Edward cursed his own negligence. All these months of routine patrols with no enemy opposition had made him careless—the worst fault of any flight commander. Now Red Flight was badly outnumbered. The enemy was suddenly out in force. *Stupid, blind idiot.*

He flung his Camel directly at the three Fokkers, causing them to swerve to avoid a collision. As the lead Jerry turned in front of him Edward pressed the trigger twice. The tracers tore through the Iron Cross on the fuselage and a line of bullet holes marched back to shatter the red tail. The Fokker wallowed in its turn, shuddered, and slipped down into a spiral. Edward had no time to watch it fall. Jeffreys was in trouble just below him, and the other three members of his flight were maneuvering desperately to try to break out of the trap.

"Dive!" Edward shouted. "Get down to the ground! You can outdive them!" The slipstream tore his words from his lips. He whipped his plane around to go to Jeffreys' aid, but the two Fokkers closed in and forced him to turn and fight.

The two enemy pilots maneuvered like veterans, and there was no way he could slip past them. No sooner had he turned to fire at one when the other was on his tail and he had to swerve away. Dully he realized that there could be only one end to this unequal duel.

His windshield shattered under a burst of machine-gun fire. He went up in a loop to get away, but he knew that he was only delaying the inevitable. At the top of the loop he saw his top wing shift alarmingly—broken spar, he thought despairingly, that tears it. No more violent maneuvers in this crate. He came down out of the loop carefully to avoid putting any extra strain on the wing. In a flash the two Fokkers were on him. It was time for the kill.

Edward watched them close in, curving to get the Camel in their sights. He felt empty, without hope, but his mind was still working. He thought of trying Doggo's diving trick to get out of a tight spot, but he knew that the wing would not take the strain. Ram one of the Jerries and take him down with him? To hell with that!

At the last minute, just as he saw the red flames leap from the muzzles of the Spandaus, he pulled the Camel up sharply. His plane lost flying speed in an instant and hung on the edge of a stall. Edward prayed fervently that the wing would stay on and that the Camel would not fall out of the stall into a fatal spin. Surprised by the unexpected maneuver, the two Fokkers sped underneath the khaki plane, their tracers whipping uselessly under its tail.

Easing the Camel out of the stall and diving to regain flying speed, Edward started a descent at full speed toward his own lines. He knew that the two enemy pilots would recover quickly and return to finish him off, but he did not care anymore. "Get it over with!" he screamed into the tearing slipstream. "Get it over with!"

He threw a quick glance back to see how long he had. To his astonishment the two Fokkers had not turned. They were speeding on! Below him the other Jerries had broken off the dogfight and were diving away! What the hell is going on? Edward wondered. His head was buzzing with bewilderment at the unexpected turn of events. *What kind of trick is this?*

Then he saw them: a dozen strange, stubby airplanes in new camouflage paint plunging down, guns chattering. One Fokker was slow to spot the newcomers, so intent was he on finishing off the elusive, crippled Jeffreys. Two of the welcome reinforcements settled quickly on the red tail, firing together. The burst shattered the Jerry's propeller, and the Fokker went down under control in a glide. The other German pilots fled at high speed.

Six of the Spads—Edward had now recognized the fluted wings and tail of the French fighter plane—took up positions around Red Flight to escort them to safety. The other six flew parallel to the new formation but five miles to the north as additional cover. Gratefully Edward waved to the pilot of the nearest Spad and received a thumb-up signal in return. At first Edward had thought Red Flight had been rescued by French pilots, but now he could see that the insignia on the fuselage was neither French nor British. Italian? No, the Italian insignia was green, white, and red. This was a five-pointed white star on a red field within a blue ring. There were no other markings except for a large letter on the tail.

They crossed the lines together at five thousand feet, then Edward signaled a course change to bring them to Saint-Omer. The strange pilot nodded and indicated that they would follow Red Flight back to the field. Low on petrol, Edward thought. Well, we'll be happy to give them some for saving our necks.

Fifteen minutes later the mechanics and off-duty pilots watched in wonder as four Camels and twelve Spads touched down and taxied up to the flight line. Edward cut his engine hastily and was out of the cockpit and running to the nearest Spad before his propeller had stopped. He was eager to know who had saved them.

A tall, lanky figure dressed in a leather flying coat and half-boots climbed down from the Spad, took off a glove, and offered his hand.

"Captain Timothy Howells, Ninety-first Aero Squadron. Hope you didn't mind our barging in like that. It didn't look like a private fight."

Edward gripped the hand vigorously and said, "My name's Burton, Number Twenty-four Squadron. Don't apologize, Captain, you were very welcome to that dogfight. We didn't know there were any Americans at the front, much less in this sector."

Howells grinned sheepishly. "Don't let my C.O. know about this, Burton. We're not supposed to be anywhere near the front. We were ferrying these planes from a factory south of Boulogne to our new base at Reims"—almost fifty miles off course, Edward thought—"when we spotted you far off. Seemed like a good chance to find out what this new model Spad could do."

They walked around the French fighter and Howells proudly explained the new design, its speed, altitude, and quickness in turns. "You can put her straight down at a hundred and sixty miles per hour and pull out as hard as you can without risking your wings. This baby is really built."

His professional pride touched, Edward asked some searching questions about engine overheating under that tight cowling and how fast the

Spad landed with those stubby wings. Meanwhile the young American pilots were slowly gathering, shaking hands, laughing and answering questions in their strange nasal accents. They looked fresh and eager and untouched by the war. Edward could not imagine wandering fifty miles off course and barging into a fight with planes they had just received and guns they had never fired. No sane British flight leader would even have considered it for a minute.

Wooley came pushing through the crowd, followed by the adjutant. Edward introduced him to Howells and briefly described how the Americans had saved Red Flight. Doggo listened gravely, then thanked the Americans for their aid and invited them for luncheon at the mess. As they set out for the mess hall Foley ordered the Spads refueled, rearmed, and inspected for battle damage before doing the same for the Camels.

"What happened to Carpenter?" the major asked Edward as they escorted Howells to the mess.

"He fell behind and the Jerries picked him off on their first pass. He went down just behind Messines." Doggo nodded sadly and was silent. *You don't have to say it, Doggo. Billy Carpenter was my responsibility and I failed him.*

Edward's gloom over the loss of his wingman soon faded. It was a merry luncheon. The Americans' high spirits were contagious, and soon the British pilots overcame their puzzlement at the strange accents and customs. There were jokes and funny toasts, songs and bawdy limericks. The cook had outdone himself to impress the visitors, and the Yanks dug in with healthy appetites. Their first taste of air combat had obviously stirred them and they had a thousand questions, some so naïve as to startle the veteran British fliers.

"How good is this new Fokker?" one Yank asked. "They didn't hang around long enough for us to find out."

Wooley grunted and twirled his wineglass thoughtfully. "Good enough. About five miles an hour faster than our Camels, climbs as well, and can turn faster than we can. A fine plane. Don't underestimate it. Worst mistake you can make."

"The Jerry pilots don't seem to be very aggressive," someone said with a New England twang. "They pulled out fast when we arrived."

Edward laughed at the naïveté of the statement. "Nine against seventeen? I'd run every time with those odds against me—if I could get away. You'll find there is very little determination to fight to the bitter end in this business. The idea is to bring down enemy machines with the least loss to your side. If by 'being aggressive' you mean sticking around regardless of the odds against you, that's stupid."

There was silence at Edward's cutting words until Jeffreys hastily interjected, "You'll have to forgive Captain Burton, chaps. He's got some of that hot American blood in him."

The tension vanished immediately, and Howells leaned over and asked what Jeffreys meant. "My father is American," Edward said, "from Philadelphia."

"The land of the bean and the cod," Jeffreys
said lightly. The Americans laughed and Howells
pointed out that that was Boston, his own home-
town. The Britishers' knowledge of the United
States was sketchy, and they had a lot of excited
questions about the American West. A young
Yank pilot held them spellbound with his descrip-
tion of the mountains, rivers, and trees of his
native Colorado. They were especially eager to
hear about the hunting: antelope, bear, buffalo—
"Not too many left these days"—and mountain
lion. The Coloradan described a hunting trip he
had made only last year where he had bagged
six deer. The British listened breathlessly to every
word.

Edward looked around the table in wonder. His
fellow pilots hunted men every day in a thousand
miles of sky and here they were listening like
schoolboys to the story of an animal hunt five
thousand miles away. Incredible. He looked across
the table at Doggo and raised an eyebrow questioningly. With a grin Wooley shrugged his shoulders and turned back to listen to the end of the tale.

The biggest laugh of the meal was garnered by
a stocky blond from New Jersey who was asked
why the United States had entered the war "rather
late in the game, old man." He stood and delivered a passionate speech to justify their presence at the front.

"Do you fellows know how many hours we've
spent in the classroom studying the English
language, English literature, and the history of

England? Hundreds and hundreds of hours memorizing Shakespeare and Milton, explaining Byron and Keats, learning the kings and queens of England from Alfred the Great to George the Fifth. Now, if you chaps lose this war, all that is wasted and we'll have to start all over again with German history, German literature, and the German language! My God, you can choke to death on those umlauts!"

The howl of laughter that greeted this sally was followed by a last round of toasts—"Easy, fellows," Howells warned, "we still have a long flight ahead of us"—and then the Americans were escorted in triumph back to the flight line. There were final handshakes, good-natured warnings about watching out for "blackbirds," and an invitation to visit the U.S. squadron at Reims. Doggo accepted for the RFC, but everyone knew that it was unlikely that the war would allow such visiting.

The Spads took off and flew east, rocking their wings in a final salute before disappearing. "Nice chaps," Jeffreys said, lighting his pipe, "but they have a lot to learn about the war in the air. They'd better lose that youthful enthusiasm fast or they won't live long enough to find out what it takes to survive out here."

Edward was annoyed at the condescending words. He had never identified himself with the States, but he liked the American pilots and was grateful for the way they had saved his flight.

"They'll learn," he said sharply, "just as we did—only faster. It's not bad to be young and enthusiastic in this stupid business. It's much worse to be old and cynical—and frightened."

Jeffreys blew into the bowl of his pipe, turned on his heel, and walked away. Doggo stood staring at the horizon where the Spads had vanished. "Good luck to them," he said. "I hear they're going into the line around Verdun."

Edward and the other pilots looked at the major in silence. Verdun was a cauldron, a continuing battle that had absorbed half the French Air Service. Losses there were the highest on the whole front. The Americans would be getting their baptism of fire; no, after today it would be their second baptism, in the furnace itself.

Edward's diary for March 18, 1918:

> Today we fought the biggest air battle of the war. At one time there were almost eighty fighters—only twenty-four of them British— in one gigantic dogfight over Le Cateau. All of Number Twenty-four was in the scrap plus six S.E. 5s from Number Forty-three at Arras. We were escorting five of the new De Havilland bombers after some bridges and roads by which the Jerries are bringing up troops and supplies for the big push. Before the first bomb was dropped we were jumped by thirty Fokker triplanes led by the Red Baron himself. Then two more *Jagdstaffels* came in: Albatroses and Pfalzes. It was a madhouse!
>
> Doggo was superb. He took on Von

Richthofen single-handed—there was no mis-
taking the Baron with that all-red Tripe of
his. Doggo fought his way through a cloud of
Fokkers, his tail protected by his wingman,
and almost nailed the Baron, but his wingman got into trouble holding off three Tripes
and Doggo had to turn away and help him.

It only lasted ten minutes but seemed like
hours. Finally both sides were low on ammunition and we were able to escape. We
lost three men: Captain Davisson, the leader
of White Flight; Lauren, a wild Welshman;
and a new man whose name I don't even
know. We also lost two S.E. 5s. The bombers
got away unscathed. Doggo shot down a
yellow and green Albatros—our only victory.

Judging from the fury of the enemy's attack and their unwillingness to let us cross
their lines, the big offensive will be any day
now.

Edward's diary for March 21, 1918:

The long-expected German offensive started
at dawn today with no preliminary bombard-
ment. There was heavy fog in the morning
and we could not take off until 1 P.M. to
strafe the advancing infantry. . . .

The Camels flew at two hundred feet above the
shell-torn ground, searching for the German shock
troops who, under the protection of the fog, had
overrun the first line of British trenches. They

swept over the stubborn little groups of English soldiers dug in to hold off the powerful enemy thrust until the front could be reestablished. Everything below was seen as if through gray-tinted glass, for the terrain was covered by a mixture of fog and the smoke of battle. It looks like a badly developed photograph of the moon, Edward thought, complete with craters. On a signal from Wooley he led Red Flight slightly to the left to give it a clear field of fire.

The Germans came out of a ruined village, bending low and spread out as skirmishers. Once again there was the hammering of machine guns, fountains of dirt leaping into the air, the crazy dancing as bullets ripped through gray-green uniforms, then the hurried enemy retreat back to the broken walls, leaving a dozen motionless figures sprawled on the road. White Flight dropped its bombs as it swept over the town, inflicting a few more casualties in its wake. The other two flights scattered to look for "targets of opportunity," as RFC Headquarters loved to call them. And in the cockpits of the Camels heads turned constantly, looking for the dreaded Fokkers.

After an hour of almost unending attacks—sometimes on a single soldier huddled in a ditch—the squadron broke off the strafing and headed home. They spotted a dogfight high over Peronne, but they were too low on fuel and ammunition to help.

As soon as they landed the mechanics swarmed over the planes to get them ready for another strafing mission. No one doubted that the orders would soon arrive for a second attack. It was clear from what they had seen that the Germans had broken through at several points and were advancing against stubborn but ineffective resistance.

Edward found Wooley gulping a cup of steaming hot tea in the operations shack. They both stared at the large map of the sector pinned to the wall. Little black arrows like darts stuck into the British positions at a hundred spots. This was where the enemy had made his deepest penetrations.

"Useless to attack just one of those points with the whole squadron," Edward noted, running his finger along the map. "Suppose we succeed in stopping them there—which is doubtful, since all they have to do is dig in and wait until we have to leave—we've accomplished nothing. Like stopping one wound when you're bleeding from a hundred. Might be better to split up into two-plane units, then we can at least delay them at a dozen places."

Doggo nodded in agreement. "It's riskier but makes more sense. Against Wing orders, of course. They think we can scare the Jerries into retreating with masses of planes diving on them at one time. Those silly blighters at headquarters even talk about the psychology of strafing. We go out this afternoon in twos. Let your flight know as soon as possible."

As Edward suspected, the new tactic only succeeded in delaying the German advance for a few hours. A twenty-mile hole had been ripped in the British lines, and the enemy was pouring men and guns into the gap. With no need to search for targets, the German fighters came down to ground level to protect their troops. The squadron lost five planes in two days of incessant fighting. One of the dead was Lieutenant Morris, whose plane was hit by ground fire. By now the airfield at Saint-Omer was within range of the enemy guns and had to be evacuated. Delayed by the inevitable morning fog, the Camels took off for the front just as the first shells exploded in the woods that bordered the field. After their fighting patrol they returned to a new base twenty miles in the rear. The great retreat had begun.

For Edward, who had taken part in the retreat in August 1914, when the Allied armies had been flung back by a seemingly invincible German horde, falling back day by day was very painful. After four years defeat was staring them in the face again. True, in 1914 the retreat had ended in the victory of the Marne, but would something like that happen now? Were the Germans likely to repeat their mistake of turning north of Paris and exposing their flank to the Anglo-French armies? "Not this time." Doggo said gloomily. "You can't hope for two miracles."

On March 25 the Germans shifted their attack south and smashed through the lines of the British Third Army. Now the whole front was wide open; it was a war of movement, not trenches. The squadron flew three missions a day, trying desperately to halt the gray-green flood. Every evening they returned to a new, hastily prepared field as the Germans marched on. The orders from

Wing became more and more strident and hysterical until Wooley refused to speak on the telephone and told his adjutant to do it.

Reinforcements arrived, new pilots fresh from England. Most of them lasted less than a week and were replaced by other bright-eyed, eager young men anxious for the thrill of battle—who were soon exhausted, gray-skinned old men with terror in their faces. Finally Wooley avoided meeting the new pilots when they arrived, and sent them directly to their flight leaders. He did not want to know what they looked like.

Sergeant-Major Foley brought two of the replacements to Edward just before dawn on the eighth day of the offensive. The introductions were brief and very military: "Lieutenants Hepburn and Ross, sir, reporting from the pilots' pool and assigned to Red Flight. Gentlemen, this is Captain Burton, your flight leader." Foley handed over the personnel orders with a sympathetic shake of his head that only Edward caught.

"Stand easy, gentlemen," Edward said as he returned the two awkward salutes. "We're not ones for military formalities up here." He riffled through the folders, noting that neither man had more than five hours in a Camel. Hepburn was eighteen years old, with a total of seventeen hours' flying time. Ross was twenty and had a grand total of fifteen hours in the air. Edward swallowed the bitterness he felt toward the men who would send such green fliers to an operational squadron in the middle of a blazing battle. The memory of Tommy Evans burned in his mind. Hepburn even looked like Tommy—sandy hair, blue eyes, strong. Ross was taller, more relaxed, seemed more sure of himself.

Which one?

To delay having to make the decision, Edward beckoned the two new pilots over to the map on the wall. "Red Flight is going out in half an hour on a strafing run here"—his finger jabbed at the map—"north of Arras. We'll be flying at less than two hundred feet to attack any German target we spot. There won't be time for any orientation flights around the sector, but it's probably just as well. Chances are we won't be landing here anyway. We've been moving back pretty steadily this past week, and by tomorrow Jerry will most likely be using this airfield. We'll be told the location of the new field before takeoff."

He paused and studied the two eager faces. *Decide. It has to be one or the other, so just make a reasonable choice. You're a flight leader, not God.*

"Lieutenant Ross will fly with us on this mission. Hepburn, get some breakfast. Then the sergeant-major will show you your quarters. And don't look so disappointed, old man"—*My God, I'm only two years older than you*—"there'll be plenty of flying for you in this war."

Ross did well, very well. Edward flew his wing and watched him carefully. The new man was a natural pilot, at ease in the air and in control of his plane at all times. Alert, too, always searching all directions for the enemy. Edward was pleased. If Ross lasted a month, he would be a first-class combat pilot.

They spotted a horse-drawn ammunition convoy on the Arras-Lens road and blew it apart in three passes. One wagon exploded just as Jeffreys's Camel was flying over it, and Edward's heart stopped as the Camel was thrown upward and banked dangerously. But Jeffreys fought the controls and pulled his plane level as the wheels almost touched the road. Ross's shooting was good, his bursts short and accurate. On the way home, Edward flew alongside the new man and gave him the thumb-up signal of approval. Ross nodded gravely and resumed his alert search of the sky. Cocky devil, Edward thought, amused. He knows how good he is. How the hell did he learn all that in fifteen hours?

That night after dinner, Major Wooley read them three "important directives" from headquarters: "One, as of April 1, 1918, the Royal Flying Corps is disbanded and will be replaced by a new independent unified service, the Royal Air Force; two, the battle is reaching its climax and squadrons are ordered to bomb and shoot anything they can see. Very low flying is essential"—"If we fly any lower," Edward shouted, "we'll need submarines, not planes"—"All risks are to be taken"—this was greeted with a howl of derisive laughter—"This order is extremely urgent"— Doggo went on, grinning at his weary fliers—"but aren't they all." There was applause, then silence as the C.O. took the third order from his jacket and looked solemnly around the mess hall. What now? Edward wondered. What else have those brass hats dreamed up for us?

Doggo cleared his throat and read slowly from the sheet. "In pursuance of Army Order 18-456, relating to Army Regulation 44-6, and with the approval of the Commander in Chief, British Expeditionary Forces in France"—he paused for maximum effect—"the shaving of the upper lip is now optional!"

They roared and pounded the tables, drank to Doggo's reddish mustache, then staggered out to their beds. Tomorrow was another day and another fight.

The next day Hepburn went down too low chasing a staff car and pulled up too late. The wing tip of his Camel touched a brick wall and the plane twisted onto its back, flattened on the road, and exploded. The squadron lost three planes that day, including one that was badly shot up and just made it back to a crash landing. The pilot had broken his leg and was dragged screaming from the wreck.

Hepburn's replacement came in late that night and was in the air the next morning. He lasted four days.

Edward's diary for April 24, 1918:

We can't go on much longer. Morale is awful, couldn't be worse. Doggo does his best but we're all worn out, men and planes, and still the Germans keep advancing. This is the third airfield we've used this week—and the worst. Everyone is in the air every day, and yet Wing keeps screaming for a greater effort, "back to the wall," "the victor is the man who lasts one hour more than his opponent," and similar bushwa. The newspapers are even worse—they make it sound as if we are winning this battle!

8

"I don't know what the bloody hell we can do more than we're doing," Captain Andrews grumbled. "We're losing men and planes faster than they're being replaced. Between the ground fire and Jerry above us, we're being shot out of the sky."

Edward and Lieutenant Collins, the new leader of White Flight, nodded their agreement. The situation in the squadron was critical. In the last ten days twelve pilots had been lost, two of them in landing accidents caused by fatigue. The Camels were long overdue for a complete overhaul, but there was no time. Battle damage had been hastily patched and the planes sent up again with broken spars held together by wire. Andrews's pale cheek twitched as he complained bitterly about engines with faulty fuel and oil lines, the lack of spare parts—particularly propellers—and outsized rounds in the gun belts that caused the machine guns to jam. "It's not the mechanics or the armorer," he said. "They're as tired as we are. No one is getting any sleep, what with this constant moving."

Wooley listened carefully, studying the faces of his flight leaders. Above his desk the bare lamp bulb cast a yellowish light that deepened the lines on the once-young faces. He's wondering how much farther he can push us, Edward thought, pitying the major. A rotten job, getting the last ounce of strength out of exhausted men. And he doesn't look too good himself. Doggo's ruddy complexion was now an unhealthy gray, and he had developed a nervous blink.

"So what do we do?" Doggo asked. There was a plaintive tone in his voice that Edward had never heard before.

No one said anything, for there was nothing to be said. They were trapped by their sense of duty, and the only thing that could be done was to go on until the last man and the last plane went down. It was stupid and illogical, but no one had a better answer. To quit was unthinkable. They were resigned to carrying out their orders until they fell. For themselves they accepted this, but for the men they led, the men who followed them loyally, seldom complaining, never shirking—that was the really hard thing to face.

"Can't we rest some of the men?" Edward asked. Wooley picked up a blue sheet from his desk and read, "Squadron maximum effort tomorrow from dawn to dusk. Enemy troops advancing toward Doullens are to be attacked at all costs. No excuses for failure will be accepted." The menacing note in the orders chilled them. For

such orders to be issued meant the battle was
being lost, perhaps even the war.

Through the window Edward could see the mechanics working feverishly in the twilight, putting
patches on bullet holes, wrapping tape around
pierced struts, pouring petrol into the tanks, and
fitting new ammunition belts. Foley was walking
up and down the line exhorting the weary men to
new efforts, warning against sloppy work. *Good
old Foley. Where would we be without him?*

"So that's it," Andrews said softly. "We begin
again tomorrow."

Throwing the orders sheet on the desk, Wooley
opened a drawer, and took out a bottle of brandy
and four glasses. He poured the drinks carefully,
not spilling a drop. "Yes," he said, "we go on. What
else can we do?"

Edward took one quick gulp from the glass,
then got up and mumbled something about seeing
to his planes. He was halfway out the door when
he heard the first bomb falling.

It started as a distant shrill whistle that grew
louder and louder until it pierced the eardrum.
The bomb exploded in the center of the airfield,
sending up a column of earth and smoke. Men
froze, then started to run blindly. Edward bolted
out of the headquarters building, followed closely
by Wooley, Andrews, and a wildly shouting Collins. Panic-stricken men ran wildly, trying to find
some spot safe from the unknown threat in the
skies.

"Gotha bombers!" Doggo shouted. "Get the men
under cover! Damn it, Sergeant-Major, stop that

panic!" Grim-faced, Foley grabbed the two nearest mechanics as they tried to run past him and dragged them to a machine-gun pit. "Get those guns firing!" he shouted. Edward peered up into the darkening sky. Useless, he thought. The Gothas are too high—can't even see them. But it keeps them busy.

The second bomb exploded next to a repair shed and in an instant turned it into a raging inferno. Sparks were blown onto the side of a temporary canvas hangar nearby. Edward spotted a group of ten men huddled behind an old stone wall. "Follow me," he shouted. "Get the planes out!" Then he ran toward the hangar without waiting to see if anyone was coming. Behind him Doggo was bellowing orders to fight the flames and cursing the frightened men shivering on the ground.

A helmeted figure in a flying jacket ran in front of Edward. A Camel was standing on the flight line, its propeller slowly ticking over. As Edward pushed hard against the door of the burning hangar he saw the lone flier climb into the cockpit, blip the engine, brake violently to clear the wheel chocks, and taxi at high speed toward the takeoff strip. Good luck, you crazy fool, Edward thought. An explosion ripped the ground not fifty feet from the careening Camel, lifting its wing dangerously, but the pilot recovered and sped down the strip and into the air.

Edward was conscious of other men helping him open the hangar doors. The air was filled with smoke and the stink of cordite. Gasping for breath, shadowy figures pushed three Camels out of the flaming hangar, dodging falling embers and yelling warnings to one another. "Watch that bloody oil, Bert!" " 'Ere, Captain, let me." One man was praying aloud, and another showed a command of profanity that excited cries of admiration from everyone but the pious soldier. As they got the third Camel safely out the roof collapsed in a river of fire, burying a fourth plane. Oil drums began to explode, and Edward ordered the men away.

A salvo of three bombs blew the operations shed apart and collapsed the end hangar. The blast knocked Edward down and he hugged the ground gratefully, out of breath. Men were screaming in pain now, and there were cries for help. It had been only two minutes since the first bomb had fallen, and the field was already a shambles. Edward looked up, searching for the brave pilot who had taken off earlier, but it was too dark now. The Gothas would be dropping their last bombs, using the burning hangar to locate the field. There was another explosion close by and Edward felt the heat, just as if someone had opened the door of a furnace. He remembered the burning Zeppelin.

Foley came running up as Edward was getting up and brushing himself off. One look at the sergeant-major's face and Edward knew it was bad.

"It's the major, sir," Foley said. "He's wounded."

Doggo was stretched out behind the stone wall with the adjutant and Andrews hovering over him. The major was covered with a blanket and only

his face, twisted by pain, showed. His breathing
was slow and laborious. As Edward hurried up
Wooley reached out and grabbed his arm, pulling
him down close to his lips. It was difficult for him
to talk.

"How bad is it, Edward?" The voice was only a
hoarse whisper. Edward looked out over the shattered field. In the light of two burning planes he
could see dark, motionless clumps that had been
men. One hangar burnt, one collapsed, fuel and
oil burning.

"Hard to tell, Doggo. It will take time to find
out." There was another explosion. Everyone but
Wooley ducked, but it was at the far end of the
field. The Gothas were finding it hard to locate the
airfield now.

"Who took off?"

Edward looked questioningly at Andrews, who
shook his head. "We don't know, old man. I
couldn't recognize his face under the goggles. I
hope he gets us a Gotha to pay for all this."

Wooley choked slightly and licked his lips.
"Brave man. See that he is decorated. Andrews,
you're senior. Take over the squadron."

Andrews patted the blanket-covered figure to
calm him. "Right. Just take it easy, old man. We'll
run things until you get back."

After two more distant explosions the raid was
over. Men got up in the darkness and looked about
in wonder. Cursing, Foley put them to work fighting the fires and pouring water on the pools of
petrol and oil. An unconscious Wooley, on a
stretcher, was loaded tenderly into the back of an

ambulance with three other casualties. The ambulance sped away to the base hospital.

"How bad is he hurt?" Edward asked.

"I can't tell, but it looks bad. He had gone into the operations room to telephone Wing, trying to get fighters sent up to cut off the Gothas on their return. The bomb buried him and we had to dig him out from a mass of rubble. His whole left side was bloody, shoulder, hip, and leg. Poor Doggo, it looks like his flying days are over."

Edward felt sick. Flying was Doggo's life, and not being able to fly would be a slow death for him. "What do we do now?" he asked, disoriented.

Andrews took out his pipe and filled it before answering. He pointed to the adjutant and said, "I want a list of all planes and pilots still fit to fly. I want it as soon as possible. Burton, check on your flight and have Collins do the same. The takeoff strip will be repaired tonight and the squadron—what's left of it—flies at dawn."

"Captain Burton, sir?" The corporal's voice was low and frightened as he tapped the shoulder of the sleeping man. Edward snarled and rolled over, burying his head under the covers.

"Sorry, sir. General Salmond's compliments and would Captain Burton report to him immediately in the major's office."

Edward sat up quickly and stared at the little corporal. "Is this a joke, corporal? If it is . . ."

"No blooming joke, sir. The general arrived half an hour ago with his whole blooming staff. He was in with Captain Andrews and the adjutant after inspecting the field, then the adjutant comes out and tells me to fetch you *toot sweet*, if you'll pardon the expression, sir."

"What time is it?"

"One fifteen, sir. Clear skies. Fresh wind from the north."

"Oh, all right, corporal. Thanks. I'll be right there."

Edward dressed hastily. A summons from the general commanding the Royal Air Force, the man who had succeeded the famous Trenchard, did not permit delay. *What the devil does he want with me? Andrews is commanding the squadron. What does he want with a flight leader? Has Masterman gotten to the general with his stories?* It certainly sounded ominous, getting him up at this hour.

When he arrived at headquarters the outer office was crowded with senior officers standing around looking as if they were attending a funeral. Masterman watched with distaste as Edward hurried into the room, then he deliberately turned his back to him, saying something to a ruddy-faced colonel at his side. The colonel stared sternly at the disheveled young captain, pointed to the undone top button on Edward's tunic, then pointed to the door to the inner office. Embarrassed and angry, Edward buttoned his tunic and smoothed his rumpled hair. *This isn't the War Office, you know. We don't have time for spit and polish here.* He knocked on the door.

"Come in." The voice was deep and noncommittal. Edward opened the door and entered.

General John Maitland Salmond, commanding the Royal Air Force, was fortyish, middle height, with shiny black hair and brown eyes. Seated behind Doggo's desk, he looked up as Edward came to rigid attention and saluted. "At ease, Burton," he said, returning the salute. "Sit down."

They looked at each other for about ten seconds, sizing each other up as soldiers do. Edward knew him to be a tough fighter with a fine tactical mind. One of the first men to join the RFC and now picked by General Trenchard as his successor.

Salmond nodded as if satisfied with something and tapped the sheet in front of him. "Burton, I'm appointing you to command the Twenty-fourth," he said, "effective immediately."

Edward stared, his mouth open. He had braced himself for a reprimand, not that he could figure out why, but he knew that Masterman did not need a reason. And instead he was being given command of the squadron!

"Sorry, sir," he said suspiciously, "I don't understand. Captain Andrews is the senior flight leader. Major Wooley specifically named him to take over."

"Captain Andrews is leaving the Twenty-fourth to take command of the Forty-eighth Squadron. This wasn't the only airfield hit by bombers, Burton. Jerry had bigger plans. He attacked four other fields. Major Popham-Smith of the Forty-eighth was killed trying to take off. All his flight leaders are too new, so I'm sending Andrews there to take charge. You'll take over here."

The piercing blue eyes searched Edward's face.

"Can you do it?" the general asked softly, rolling
a pen between his fingers.

Edward thought of Fortescue and Wooley. He
remembered what the torture of command had
done to both of them, the way they had changed,
the loneliness, anguish, and pain of giving orders
that inevitably meant death to others. It had killed
Fortescue and changed Doggo from a close friend
to a worn-out heavy drinker. Could he handle the
pressures any better? He wasn't a better man or a
better flier than they, why would it be any different for him? He stalled for time.

"I'd like to think it over, sir."

Salmond shook his head emphatically. "The
situation is critical, Burton. The enemy is advancing daily and our troops are spent. Jerry has over
a hundred divisions brought in from the Russian
front, and he's throwing them at us without regard
to losses. This is his last hope and he knows it. If
he reaches Paris, he wins the war. If not—if we
can stop him and re-form the front—he inevitably
loses as the Americans pour in. Everything depends on the next hour, the next day, the next
week. The men, exhausted as they are, must be
pushed until they fall. It's a brutal task for a
commanding officer. Can you do it?"

And if not me, Edward thought, who? Collins?
Would he do better? Probably not with that hasty
temper of his. Someone from another squadron?
A stranger? Edward winced.

"Do tomorrow's orders still stand, sir?" Edward
asked. He searched desperately for an excuse to

refuse, anything to get out of the net Salmond was spinning about him.

The general nodded gravely. "Every plane in the air at dawn. I've already telephoned the depot. Reinforcements will arrive by ten o'clock, but you will have every plane flyable attacking the Doullens road by then. Sorry, Burton, there are no time-outs for injuries in this bloody game. Well?" Salmond fingered the appointment orders on the desk. *He's beginning to think he made a mistake.*

"I'll do my best, sir." *We all do our best, even you, sir. You push C.O.'s into the grinding machine and I do it to the pilots. What does that make us?*

Salmond sighed and slumped back into his chair. "Thank you, Burton. I know you will. Masterman warned me against appointing you, but 'Boom' Trenchard had a long talk with me before he left to command this new independent bombing force. He handed me a list of men he had been keeping an eye on, men he considered qualified to command squadrons. Your name was near the top of the list. I won't read you the comments he had scribbled in opposite your name, but they were very flattering. I'm certain that you can do the job."

Then you're surer of it than I am, Edward thought. *But I have to try. No one knows the squadron better than I do. For what that's worth in this hellish business.*

The general signed the appointment orders and slid the papers across the desk. Edward pocketed them, stood up, and saluted. Salmond wished him luck, then said, "By the way, Burton, the pilot who took off after the Gothas—Lieutenant Ross?—he caught up with them as they were pounding the Twenty-seventh at Amiens. Unfortunately his plane had not been rearmed. His gun belts were empty."

Edward's head reeled. He knew what was coming even before the general said it. "We've just received a telephone call from Amiens. They found the wreckage of a Gotha in a field near the town. The remains of the Camel were mixed in with it. Ross had rammed the Jerry and gone down with it. I'm recommending him for the Victoria Cross."

On the way out Edward found the adjutant chatting with a staff major. He cut their conversation short, ignoring the pained look on the flunky's face. "After the general leaves," Edward ordered firmly, "report to my quarters with the engineering officer. Bring the squadron roster and the latest status report. Tell the sergeant-major I want to see him in an hour. Breakfast at 4:30 A.M., briefing at 5:00. The squadron flies at first light. That's all."

They hit the crowded Doullens road in waves, blasting everything within range of their guns. Edward led the first attack up the center of the jam-packed road, firing steadily. He circled widely as Collins's flight bombed in turn. Blue Flight was led by Lieutenant Ernest Fredericks, a tough, no-nonsense Australian, who was Edward's first

appointment as C.O. After hammering what remained standing on the road, his Camels switched
their fire to the Germans huddled in the ditches.
When Fredericks was done, Edward brought Red
Flight down again. The ground fire was murderous, but the Camels stubbornly bore in, disregard-
ing their losses. One Camel exploded over the
truck column. Another crash-landed in a field,
and Edward saw Germans running from the
ditches toward the wreck. In a flash Fredericks
and his wingman dove on them, guns blazing, and
sent them sprawling. The downed pilot fired his
pistol into the cockpit of his plane, waited until
smoke poured out, then fled into the woods. Good
man, Edwards thought. Then he signaled the
squadron to re-form and head for home.

"Yes, Sergeant-Major?"
"Replacements, sir. Three planes and pilots.
Just reported in from the depot."
Edward groaned and looked despairingly across
the room at Lieutenant Thomas, his balding, over-
weight adjutant. "Three planes? We lost six planes
and two pilots in the air raid, and two more this
morning. Call Wing, Thomas, and tell them we
are down to nine aircraft—including the replacements. Even those fools must know we can't stand
these losses without more men and planes."
Before the worried adjutant could reach for
the telephone, it rang loudly. "Wing calling, sir.
They want to know why the squadron is not back
in the air."

"Tell them the pilots are playing three chukkers of polo for the championship of northwest France and can't be disturbed."

The adjutant murmured something calming into the telephone and hung up. "They sounded pretty upset, sir," he said. Edward frowned and made a rude noise with his lips.

"How soon, Sergeant-Major?"

"Fifteen minutes, sir. They're refueling the last planes now."

"All pilots in the briefing room immediately."

"Yes, sir." Foley snapped to attention, turned smartly, and marched out at a quick step. Edward watched him affectionately until the door closed. *What we would do without Foley to remind us that we're soldiers?*

"Thomas." The adjutant came to the desk and stood waiting. "Call the base hospital at Amiens in an hour and find out how Doggo is doing. They're operating on his hip right now. And Thomas . . ."

"Sir?"

"If I don't get back, there is a letter in this desk drawer that I want you to mail. Understood?"

The adjutant stiffened with surprise. A non-flying officer commissioned directly from civilian life, he clearly felt that this was not the proper attitude for a squadron commander to have before going into action. "I'm certain you'll be back, sir."

Edward managed a smile in spite of his fatigue. "Well, one never knows. Wish me luck."

"Good luck, sir."

The telephone again rang shrilly. Edward got up and walked to the door.

"Tell them to go to hell," he said over his shoulder, "because that's where they're sending us."

The door closed and the troubled adjutant slowly picked up the telephone.

"Twenty-four Squadron. Yes, sir, they're on their way."

Edward's diary for May 23, 1918:

> Now I know what keeps men going day after day even when they are exhausted. Not King and Country, the Flag, the Righteousness of Our Cause—they jeer at that. No, it is much simpler: loyalty to the small group of men with whom one daily faces death. It's the other pilots in the flight, sometimes the squadron, but never any larger outside group. This loyalty is so intense, so all-important, that a man will gladly risk being killed or wounded rather than see contempt in the eyes of his own little 'band of brothers.' He'll drag himself to his plane when every fiber of his being screams for relief from the terror of combat flying.
>
> I've ordered the pilots to be quartered together by flight and to be seated together by mess. Anything to foster this bond. Strange that Allen and Doggo did not recognize this loyalty. It would have made their jobs easier and saved them much pain.

If this works, I will have mastered the job of commanding officer of a squadron.

In June and July the Germans made their last effort—and failed. Fresh, unblooded American troops had been rushed into the line to plug the gaps. Along with the stubborn British and French divisions they stopped the enemy short of Paris and, for the first time, threw them back. The war was won. Now it was only a question of time.

In the air the tide of battle also turned. Wing ordered an end to strafing and a return to high-altitude offensive patrols to sweep the skies of enemy fighters. German observation planes were to be the main target—blinding the Jerries to the Allied preparations for the advance. "Ruthless determination" was called for; bone-tired pilots laughed bitterly and went out to find the enemy. Under strength, their planes worn out, the squadrons fought on.

In the beginning of July, Edward was promoted to major and ordered home on leave. The order was signed by the commanding general himself. Two weeks' leave starting immediately.

9

The couple left the cool greenness of the park for the bright sunlight of Park Lane. Ann clung to his arm, as if afraid he might vanish again. There were still touches of her illness in her face and she tired easily, but these walks alone together were the happiest part of the day for them. Since he had arrived to find her waiting on the railroad platform, they had talked incessantly: about the war, their misunderstanding, Doggo and the squadron, Iain, wartime London, but mostly of themselves—what they felt and what they feared. It had come as a shock to Edward that they had not seen each other for almost two years. There was so much to talk about and so little time.

London was a dismal gray, clearly showing the strains of the war. Men had marched through these streets in August 1914 with the bright colors of flags and uniforms sparkling, drums and trumpets sounding their call to arms, off to fight but promising to be home by Christmas. Four

years of long casualty lists had left the city sunk
in apathy. Widow's weeds and black armbands
were everywhere. Wounded men, the lucky ones,
hobbled on crutches or were guided by nurses. An
older man with an empty left sleeve and a black
eye-patch gravely raised his hat as he passed Edward in the park. Edward saluted, standing at
attention. The mutilated man smiled at Ann and
passed on.

They stood on the hot street corner, reluctant
to return to the Ogilvie house and surrender their
privacy. Thomas Ogilvie and the servants meant
well and they were terribly proud of "the major,"
but Ann sensed that Edward was uncomfortable
with all the attention. She had dissuaded her
father from giving a large dinner party to intro-
duce Edward to family friends, saying that he
needed rest and quiet. They spent most of their
evenings alone in the living room talking, sharing.

Yesterday they had taken the train down to
Sussex to visit Doggo. The convalescent hospital
was a large red Georgian manor hidden in the
depths of a wooded park. Doggo had been waiting
for them at the gate. Even in the wheelchair he
looked as bluff and hearty as ever. They had spent
the whole afternoon laughing over old jokes and
remembering old friends.

Ann was instantly accepted into the privacy of
their friendship, for she was not only Edward's
fiancée but Iain's sister and therefore doubly
joined to the squadron. Before they left, Edward
spoke to Doggo's doctor, who pointed out that
Major Wooley was lucky to have kept his right

leg—the knee and hip had been badly shattered. "He'll be fortunate if he walks again, much less fly" was the grim verdict. Doggo had often told Edward that he planned to make a career in the Royal Air Force after the war.

A well-dressed young man crossed the street and stood near them, waiting for a bus. Edward stared at him curiously. It was rare to see a healthy young man not in uniform, but there was no hostility in Edward's look. Good luck to him, he thought sadly. He's better off out of it.

From the shadows of the park an elderly woman darted out, grabbed the lapel of the young man's jacket, and thrust a white feather into the buttonhole. " 'Ere," she snarled, " 'at's for them that won't fight for their country." She darted away.

Red with embarrassment, the young man fingered the feather and stared after the fleeing figure. There was a sickly grin on his lips as he looked pleadingly about. Ann walked over to him, pulled the feather from his lapel, and threw it into the gutter. "That old hag should have her face slapped," she said. Edward nodded, but he felt uncomfortable.

"It does seem a bit much," the young man murmured. "I tried to enlist several times, but they keep telling me I'm in a reserved category—essential war work, more important than being in the trenches."

He was a chemist, he explained, working at a government laboratory in Hounslow. Very secret stuff—new high explosives and things like that. His superior had told him to stop making a nuisance of himself with his applications to enlist and to get on with his work. "He said I was worth much more to the war at my desk than in France."

Shaking his head at the injustice of it all, he tipped his hat and walked dejectedly down the street. Edward wondered at the new, ugly mood he sensed in the country.

As they strolled back to the house they passed two American officers—fliers, judging by the wings on their tunics—who saluted smartly and smiled approvingly at Ann. Edward returned the salute, piqued at the attention they were paying to his girl. But he laughed and told Ann about the Americans who had saved Red Flight and about the hilarious luncheon in the mess. They laughed together over their explanation of why they were in the war—"Don't want to start learning German, they said." He did not repeat the ribald jokes and limericks. He still felt shy about discussing with Ann anything that hinted of sex, although he knew that her job as a nurse's aid in the hospital must have taught her much. Perhaps his reticence had something to do with Yvette, a fear that he might blurt out the truth about that night in Amiens. *But I thought I had lost you forever.*

The two weeks passed quickly, and as Edward packed his kit on the last day he was astonished to find that he was anxious to get back to the squadron. London had depressed him. As much as he loved Ann and wanted to be with her, he had the nagging feeling that he was needed in France. Responsibility of command, team spirit,

comradeship—call it what you will, he thought,
I've got to get back and help.

Ann drove him to Dover in the family Daimler
and walked with him arm in arm onto the ferry
slip. At the last checkpoint they said good-bye
among a hundred other couples, all whispering,
kissing, clinging together—all with the same
thought: Is this the last time? The military police
looked on with a sympathetic air.

Whistles blew. It was time to go.

Edward kissed Ann, then held her at arm's
length and looked carefully at her tearful face.
"Good-bye, my dearest Ann," he said. "Remember
one thing always. I'm coming back."

Then he grabbed his musette bag and ran to
the gangplank. He did not look back. It would
have been too painful. In the smoky ship's lounge
he found a seat against a bulkhead and, following
the good soldier's first rule, went to sleep.

Edward's diary for September 12, 1918:

Eight new Camels arrived today, bringing us
up to strength for the first time since March.
Three of the new pilots are old-timers who
have been at the front before. Even the others
are better trained, more alert, more realistic
than before. One of them actually has
twenty-five hours in a Camel!

Foley warned me that the men are beginning to resent the tight discipline I've im-
posed since I returned from leave, but it is

essential to keep the squadron at maximum
efficiency. Yesterday I put a mechanic on report for using a dirty chamois filter cloth
while refueling a plane. That could mean an
engine failure from a dirty carburetor. Today
I took White Flight away from Collins and
will recommend that he not be made captain. Against strict orders he led the flight
down to attack some Fokkers instead of protecting the observation planes. While he was
shooting down one Jerry, seven Albatroses
got two of the Bristol two-seaters. Sheer
stupidity in a flight leader.

Remington, the military correspondent of
The Times, arrived unexpectedly today. We
had a marvelous talk.

"I'm surprised, Major," Henry Remington said,
"that they let you command a squadron at the
front after the blasting you gave them in that
interview."

Edward grinned and refilled the older man's
glass. They were seated in the C.O.'s office and
chatting in a relaxed, informal way. The adjutant
had strict orders not to interrupt except in an
emergency.

"I'm surprised, Mr. Remington, that they let
you come to the front, considering the blasting
you give them every day."

The military expert waved his cigar and chuck-
led. "One has friends, of course, and *The Times*
is not without influence in high places. But you
didn't get your rank and command by pulling

strings. I hear that General Masterman is still after your head."

"The worst he can do is take away my rank and my job—and I'd thank him for it. It's a lot easier just flying and fighting."

"You've had more than your share of both," Remington said thoughtfully. "Over four years. By the way, you must be doing a fine job with the squadron. I heard in the halls of the War Office last week that you're to be given the D.S.O. A major, a squadron commander at the front, *and* the Distinguished Service Order—that is a record to be proud of. And you're only twenty."

Edward twisted uncomfortably in his chair. Talk of his accomplishments always made him nervous. He could not help thinking of all the friends he had lost on his way up. Also, it was bad luck to boast like that. Don't tempt the gods, Doggo used to say. They're jealous.

Remington saw the look on Edward's face and changed the subject quickly. "The Americans are attacking in the Meuse-Argonne sector today. If they're successful, that should take a lot of pressure off you. The Germans will have to shift some of their best squadrons to Alsace to stop them, don't you think?"

"The Jerries will find that difficult. We're doing more than just holding our own here. We keep up a constant pressure, more offensive patrols, more raids on their airfields, more strafing of their trenches, to make them come up and fight. They're not the same men we faced last year, the German pilots. They've lost too many of the veterans, and their replacements are ill-trained. They can't afford to weaken their strength in this sector too much or we'll drive them out of the skies."

There was a note of pride in Edward's voice that the correspondent noted carefully. They had told him that morale in the RAF had improved drastically, but he had not believed it until now. Unbelievable! Twenty-year-old majors leading sixteen planes and pilots to battle every day. Who would have thought it possible?

Remington knocked the ash from his cigar and picked up the conversation again. "I saw Rudyard Kipling last month. Went down to offer my condolences on the loss of his son at the front. Poor fellow is taking it very hard. Some harpy sent him a letter gloating over the boy's death, blames Rudyard for being a jingo and wanting this war. Well, he was very glad to see me and we sat and talked for hours after dinner. He hates this war, keeps talking about Armageddon, poison gas, and airplanes. Thinks the Germans will get desperate and flood the cities with gas from the sky, avoid defeat by terror. Is that possible?"

"Yes and no. Yes, they could spray poison gas over London, but I doubt if they have enough long-range planes to have much effect. Also, they would worry about retaliation. Bombs, especially incendiaries, would be better. Start a lot of fires. Burn out the city." Edward's cold, matter-of-fact voice disturbed the older man.

"That's a horrible thought," Remington said, pushing his drink aside. Edward shrugged his shoulders and stared coldly across the desk. *But*

*this is the way we soldiers make our livings, Mr.
Military Expert.*

"Yes," he said, "I agree. The choice between
choking to death slowly and being torn to pieces
in a fraction of a second is a horrible one, but the
end result is the same."

He pushed Remington's glass back until it
touched the correspondent's fingers. "Tell Mr.
Kipling that he won't see it in this war—not time
enough; but he'd better start worrying about the
next one."

"The next one?"

Edward's smile was tight-lipped. "Jerry has lost
this one, but I'll wager that right now their High
Command is planning for the next war. Then
you'll see airplanes and bombing come into its
own. It will make this war look like a church
bazaar."

"It's started already," Remington said quietly.
"Last week fourteen German bombers hit London
in broad daylight. Civilian casualties were high,
and the brutes even hit a wing at Chelsea Hospital."

Edward froze. Ann was a nurse at Chelsea.

The correspondent saw the stricken look on the
younger man's face and hastily added, "No nurses
were injured, Major. Your friend Miss Ogilvie was
very brave. She led the evacuation of the blind
patients out of the ward through a burning corridor. A splendid young woman. She'll get the
George Medal for that day's work."

Edward swallowed his drink and asked hoarsely,
"How did you know that Ann and I . . . ?"

Remington smiled. "Thomas Ogilvie and I have been good friends since we starved together on field duty in South Africa. I've known Ann and Iain since they were children."

There was a timid rapping on the door. Thomas peered into the room and said apologetically, "Sorry, sir, but you did say an emergency. Wing is on the telephone. Enemy aircraft reported over Arras—about ten fighters and bombers. All planes to intercept immediately."

"Is White Flight back yet?" The adjutant shook his head.

"All right, alert Red and Blue flights. I'll see them in the briefing room immediately. I'll lead."

Thomas disappeared hastily. Edward rose from behind the desk, took his helmet and goggles from the wall, and stared at the operations map, figuring out courses, speeds, and altitudes. Then he remembered his guest.

"Sorry about this," he said, smiling. "But do stay for dinner. We're having mutton—I think. You can meet the other chaps and we can talk some more."

With an airy wave of the hand he left the office. On the flight line engines were sputtering to life as the mechanics went through the preflight checks. Foley came running up. "Ten planes, sir. Number five Camel has a broken cylinder rod."

"Oh, very well, Sergeant-Major. We'll be taking off as soon as the pilots are assembled." Number five was a new man named Reeves. Well, he's out of it—just as well.

* * *

They found the enemy making his last sweep over the smoking rubble of the Abbeville railroad yards—four Gotha bombers at five thousand feet covered by six Fokkers at nine. Edward gave the go-ahead signal to Jeffreys, and Blue Flight slanted down to attack the bombers. When the Fokkers spotted the diving planes and turned to intercept them, Edward thrust his gloved hand high above his head, pushed the control stick full forward, and sent the Camel into a screaming dive. Behind him the rest of Red Flight followed. *Perfect. The sun is behind us.*

Unaware of the threat diving on them, the Fokkers were banking sharply to follow the five audacious Camels that swept past them toward the bombers. At one hundred yards, Edward pressed the trigger, the lead Fokker dead in his gunsight. The tracers leaped across space and buried themselves in the black and yellow fuselage, then climbed quickly up to the cockpit. The pilot never turned as his plane flopped over on its back and began a slow spin to the ground. Five against five—even odds.

The dogfight lasted about ten minutes as two more Fokkers went down, one of them a flamer. Edward followed one of the remaining Jerry planes, which was diving frantically, trying to escape. An amateur, Edward thought contemptuously, trying to outdive a Camel. He did not bother to look back. He knew his wingman was there covering his tail. Two of the four Gothas were down and Jeffreys was chasing the other two.

The Fokker leveled off at three hundred feet

and banked sharply, trying to throw off the Camel that clung to its tail. Tracers tore through its right wing and the German pilot flung the plane into an opposite bank to get away from the fatal yellow lines. In his terror he pushed rudder too hard, causing the gaily painted Fokker to skid dangerously and lose altitude. My God, Edward thought, horrified, he can't even fly. Then he saw the enemy pilot pounding on his machine guns. *Jammed.*

The Fokker's cockpit filled Edward's gunsight. He had only to touch the trigger and the man ahead was dead. But he hesitated—not out of chivalry; those days were long gone. It was a sudden anger, a hot flush of refusal to murder a man because it was his duty.

The German looked back, his face a white mask beneath his goggles. Edward pointed to the left, toward the Allied lines. Relieved, the enemy pilot waved his gloved hand, then saluted. The Fokker banked left as the two Camels took up position on either side and to the rear. Swiftly the odd three-plane formation flew at low altitude over the British trenches as the troops looked up and cheered. High overhead eight Camels followed them home.

The Fokker landed first, with Edward and his wingman directly behind him. When the enemy plane arrived at the tarmac, Foley and an armed guard were waiting. The sergeant-major saluted politely—an enemy officer was still an officer and entitled to military courtesy—and invited "Herr

Leutnant" to step down. Then he had the plane
thoroughly searched for booby traps. Military
courtesy was one thing; military stupidity another.

By the time Edward clambered down from his
cockpit and ran over to the Fokker, Remington
was speaking quietly to the German flier, who was
leaning against his plane, pale and frightened.
Around them a smiling, laughing mob of pilots
and mechanics were admiring the trophy and
staring curiously at its pilot. "God," one man said,
" 'e ain't but a kid."

"Sergeant-Major!" Edward's voice was angry,
and the crowd froze. "Escort the prisoner to my
office and send these men back to their duties."
With a jerk of his chin Edward told Remington
to follow him and act as translator.

Leutnant Wilhelm Doenitz was, in fact, seventeen, and had been assigned to *Jagdstaffel* 18 at
Douai just three days before. This had been his
first trip over the lines. He had been told by his
flight leader to dive for home at the first sign of
trouble, but it had all happened too quickly. The
flight leader had been the first to fall, then Doenitz
had become confused. The next thing he remembered, he had been in a dive with Edward on his
tail. The German looked almost terrified. Remington spoke to him soothingly and got a long,
rambling reply. The correspondent bit his lip, then
said, "They told him that the British are butchers
and took no prisoners. He thinks we are going to
shoot him after the questioning."

Edward took Doggo's brandy and three glasses

from his desk drawer. He filled the glasses, handed one to the German, one to Remington, and raised his own in a toast. "Tell him that we never shoot men we have drunk with. Ask him if he'll drink this toast: to hell with the war and all generals." Remington translated and the German flier grinned weakly and raised his glass. They all drained their glasses.

For the next hour they sat in Edward's office, sipping the brandy and talking about the war. Relieved of his fear, Doenitz was eager to speak, sometimes even letting slip an important bit of military information, like the location of his squadron and which new model fighter they had been promised. Remington translated Edward's sour comment that headquarters on both sides of the lines were always promising newer, faster planes, and the German dutifully grinned.

Less than a year ago, Doenitz had been a high school student in Mainz, a high-spirited, patriotic youth eager to serve the Fatherland. He had always been fascinated by airplanes and had often cut class to sneak down to the army airfield on the outskirts of the town to watch the training flights take off and land. It had been the death of his hero, Von Richthofen, in April that had compelled him to enlist. "I had this idea that I would be the one to avenge him—shoot down the English pilot who had killed the great German ace." Remington smiled as he translated the naïve remark, but Edward nodded thoughtfully. He understood Doenitz. How could he not understand why a sixteen-year-old schoolboy, a little wild, mad about airplanes, would lie about his age to get into the Great Adventure? Four years ago he had done the same thing. And how many other schoolboys had followed the same path—on both sides—and were now buried in little cemeteries near their airfields? And how many more were still to fall if this damned war was not ended?

There was a timid knock on the door. The adjutant came in at Edward's command to announce that the escort had arrived to take the prisoner to Wing.

Edward's diary for October 23, 1918:

> Rain showers and low clouds. No flying today. The war news is good on all fronts. The enemy is falling back stubbornly, but still falling back. We are beginning to sense victory in the air. The amount of paperwork necessary to run this squadron is unbelievable. . . .

"Yes, Sergeant-Major, what is it?"

"It's Corporal Martin, sir. He's had a letter today from his mother saying that his wife is running around with men and neglecting the children. He's in a very bad state, Martin is."

"Damn it, Sergeant-Major, you saw the directive from Wing. There is to be no leave granted for any reason until further notice."

"Yes, sir, I saw it, but I'm that concerned about Martin."

"How long since Martin's been home?"

"Seventeen months, sir."

"My God! No wonder his wife is seeing other men. Thomas! Make out orders for Corporal Martin to proceed without delay to RAF Supply, London, for two weeks' instruction in the maintenance of new-type Mark V magnetos. Top priority. Lay on some transportation for him, Sergeant-Major. If he makes the midnight leave ship from Calais, he'll be in London by dawn."

"Yes, sir, and may I thank the major—"

"No, you may not, but you may tell Martin that if he kills anyone in the next two weeks, I'll be in a great deal of trouble. That's all."

"Sir!"

"Lieutenant Oliver reporting for duty, sir."

"At ease, Oliver. Welcome to Twenty-four Squadron. Have a nice trip?"

"Oh yes, sir, but I was very anxious to get here. I've heard a great deal about this squadron and especially about you, sir."

"Oh, have you? And what have you heard and from whom?"

"From the headmaster at Falkland School, sir, just before I left to enlist. He gave a talk to the whole school about the old boys who had gone off to fight the day war was declared. He's very proud of you, sir; holds you up as an example to the rest of us. I remember his reading off a list of the

former students, their present ranks, their com-
mands, and their decorations. Your name was
first."

"Was it? Did he mention names like Colley
Evans?"

"I don't believe so."

"Arthur Bendon, Louis Enstone, Tommy Evans,
Martin Hyde, or Richard Makepeace?"

"Uh, no, sir, he did not."

"No, I didn't think he would. He probably
lumped them all together under the anonymous
heading of 'the honored dead.' The sergeant-major
will show you to your quarters, Lieutenant, then
report to Captain Jeffreys. I strongly suggest that
you listen very carefully to everything he will tell
you and follow his orders to the letter. If you do,
you stand a fair chance of staying off the Head's
list of losers."

"Yes, sir. Thank you, sir."

Edward's diary for November 5, 1918:

We returned to the old airfield at Saint-Omer
this morning. Jerry had kept it nice and
clean for us. No booby traps—he's falling
back too quickly for that. Our armies are
advancing on all fronts against stubborn resistance. It can't be too much longer.

The signs multiplied that the war was coming
to an end. Germany's allies deserted her and sued
for peace. Through neutral countries came reports

of food riots and street fighting in Berlin, mutiny in the Imperial German Navy—then a rumor that the Kaiser had abdicated and fled to Holland.

On the ground the enemy armies retreated slowly, stubbornly exacting a bloody toll for every inch they yielded. In the air the German pilots fought with the desperation of men facing inevitable defeat, but they were no longer the feared veterans of a year ago.

The long-awaited end was imminent—but when?

He was reading a letter from Ann when the telephone rang, breaking his concentration. The adjutant was out of the office, so Edward picked it up and said in an annoyed voice, "Twenty-four Squadron. Major Burton." He listened expressionless to the breathless, excited voice of the Wing operations officer, trying to focus on the rapid words. But the blood began to pound in his ears and his eyes were smarting. It was hard to grasp. It had been expected, but somehow he had been afraid to believe it. He cleared his throat.

"Yes, sir, I understand; 11:00 A.M. Yes, it's marvelous news. I'll let the men know at once. And thank you, sir."

He put down the telephone slowly and wiped his eyes on his sleeve. Outside the headquarters building he found Foley talking to the armorer.

"Sergeant-Major." Foley stiffened to attention, alerted by the break in the C.O.'s voice. "The squadron is to stand down. All patrols are canceled. An armistice has been signed and all hostilities cease at 11:00 A.M. Pass the word on, please. And the squadron will assemble at ten for a memorial service for our dead. That's all."

An hour later they stood together, heads bared in the chill wind, among the broken propellers that marked the graves in the little cemetery. Officers and men still dazed by the news stared down at the brown hummocks covered with the red and yellow leaves of autumn. As the chaplain droned on, talking of courage and sacrifice, Edward looked down the line, seeing the wonder in each man's face. They still can't grasp the idea that they've survived, he thought, that the war is over and they'll be going home instead of resting here with so many others. He had not been listening to the sermon, but the padre suddenly ended with a line from the *Iliad* that Edward remembered from his Greek class—how many years ago? "They perished in Troy, far from their beloved native land." Someone behind Edward was sobbing, and someone else was cursing under his breath. Edward nodded to the officer in charge of the ceremonial firing squad.

A volley split the air, and startled blackbirds exploded from the nearby woods. The bugler sounded "Last Post." Everyone came to attention and saluted. It was over. They had said their last good-bye to their departed comrades.

As they marched back to the airfield Edward told Foley to have his plane warmed up. The sergeant-major looked at him strangely, but said nothing.

* * *

He flew directly to Mons, with its canal and wheat fields, and said good-bye to the sixteen-year-old who had seen the great battle here from the observer's cockpit of a flimsy Farman pusher plane. Then he found the riverbank where Iain had jumped to his death, and he said good-bye to his best friend. There were ruined villages, abandoned trenches, rusty lines of barbed wire, even old airfields that he knew better than he knew the streets of London. Here he had gotten his first victory, an Aviatik, with the machine gun that Iain had fitted to the Farman despite the predictions of disaster. Here they had lost Weston, killed on his first flight over the lines. There was the road where Allen had dived into a truck. There were so many he had to say good-bye to.

He flew low over the trenches, enjoying the unusual sensation of not ducking ground fire. Soldiers were standing on the parapets, staring across the shell-torn battleground. Even now they did not dare step forward into no-man's-land, where only this morning it would have been suicide to cross. They just gazed, silent, unbelieving, at the enemy. It was ten minutes past eleven.

Ann came to his mind, a sweet, comforting thought. He concentrated on her—and what his future would be. It had to include flying, for he had never lost his love of the air even in the depths of the worst battles. Should he stay in the Royal Air Force? With his war record it was very tempting, but he did not think he would fit into the peacetime service. He thought of Doggo and winced.

He would marry Ann and find a job flying. That was as far ahead as he could see.

The Camel flew along on its pilgrimage. Suddenly, over the red roofs of Lille, Edward spotted a Fokker coming toward him. Automatically he leaned forward to arm his guns, then relaxed with a sour grin. *No more of that. It's over. Just another pilot saying good-bye to his old battlefields.* They passed at a hundred yards and saluted each other gravely. Then the Fokker was gone.

Before he knew it, the familiar crisscross pattern of the landing strips at Saint-Omer was under his wing. He pressed the interrupter button to idle the engine and slipped down to his last wartime landing. Four years, three months, six days . . . a lifetime.

As he taxied up to the tarmac Foley was standing there, watching and waiting. The Camel swung around to line up with the other planes. It stood there for a long minute, its propeller idly ticking over.

Exhausted, Edward sat in the cockpit, his head lowered. It was hard to realize that there would be no more patrols, no more losses, no more empty chairs in the mess each night. Something sparkled on the instrument panel—the silver medallion of Saint Jude that Mr. Ogilvie had given him. He pried it off and pocketed it.

Switch off. The propeller arc disappeared, and the blades slowed and stopped. The engine coughed once and was silent.

The war was over.

About the Author

Milton Dank grew up in Philadelphia and attended the University of Pennsylvania, from which he holds a doctorate in physics. During World War II he served as a glider pilot in Europe and has been an enthusiastic flyer ever since. After the war, Mr. Dank worked as a research physicist in the aerospace industry.

Mr. Dank's most recent book for Delacorte was *Khaki Wings*, in which the story of Edward Burton was begun. The author has also written nonfiction books about World War II, as well as two earlier novels for young adults about the French Resistance, *The Dangerous Game* (available in a Dell Laurel-Leaf edition) and its sequel, *Game's End*.

Mr. Dank lives with his family in Wyncote, Pennsylvania.